ABOUT THE SPARTAPU

"Cattastic" – LONDON EVENIN(

"A highly original story with lots of scope for giggles, it also provides some background history and can't fail to delight cat fans (or otherwise) everywhere!'
– BOOKTRUSTED.CO.UK

"Non-stop adventure... Spartapuss serves notice that cattitude rules!" – I LOVE CATS (USA)

"Packed with more catty puns than you ever thought pawsible, this witty Roman romp is history with cattitude." – SCHOLASTIC JUNIOR MAGAZINE

"...the descriptions of life in classical Rome are good, particularly the set piece in the Arena...Readers who know the original stories will enjoy the fun, and those who don't know the history may be enticed to look more closely at the Roman stories."– THE SCHOOL LIBRARIAN, VOL 53

"This is too good to be left just as a children's book! Extremely funny and brilliantly written..."
– MONSTERS AND CRITICS.COM

"I would recommend them... Thrillers that you can't put down 'til you've read the whole thing."
– FIONA MURRAY THE JOURNAL OF CLASSICS TEACHING

JOIN THE FELINE EMPIRE AT
WWW.SPARTAPUSS.CO.UK

LAND OF
THE KITONS

PURRMANIA

NEUTERBERGER
FOREST

MAUL

HISSPANIA

ROME

CATTAGE

LAND OF THE
KUSHONITES

THE FELINE
EMPIRE

MOUNT
OLYMPUSS

TRAY

THE SQUEAK ISLANDS

MISR
(FLEAGYPT)

The Spartapuss Series

I Am Spartapuss (Book I) ISBN: 9781906132422
Catligula (Book II) ISBN: 9781906132484
Die Clawdius (Book III) ISBN: 9780954657680
Boudicat (Book IV) ISBN: 9781906132019
Cleocatra's Kushion (Book V) ISBN: 9781906132064

The Olympuss Games Series

Son of Spartapuss (Book I) ISBN: 9781906132811
Eye of the Cyclaw (Book II) ISBN: 9781906132835
Maze of the Minopaw (Book III) ISBN: 9781906132842
Stars of Olympuss (Book IV) ISBN: 9781906132828

I AM SPARTAPUSS

ROBIN PRICE

MOGZILLA

For Scarlet...

I AM SPARTAPUSS

First published by Mogzilla in 2004
Paperback edition published in 2005
This edition published in 2016.

ISBN: 9781906132422

Printed and bound in the UK by CPI Group.

The author would like to thank the following: Michele, Peter, Hayley,
Christina G, Sam, Phil, Annabel, Rupert, Nick, Ricky, John G, Sinc,
Andrew, Bev, Les, Kirsty, Claire E, Twiz, Ed, Arvind, Tanuja, Jon,
Olivia, Am, Ben, David, Mum and Dad, Nicole, Catherine B,
Nicholas R, Guy G, Caroline C and Rupert.

DRAMATIS PAWSONAE

Who's who!

Rome AD 36. The Feline Empire rules the known world

Cats of the Imperial family:

Tiberius – The Emperor. Nickname: 'Tibbles'.
Mewlia – The Emperor's ageing mother.
'Catligula' – Mewlia's great-grandson. Real name
Gattus Tiberius. Spoilt from the litter!
Clawdius – Catligula's uncle (and Mewlia's
grandson). Owner of Spatopia, Rome's Finest
Bath and Spa.

Slaves, strays and other animals:

Spartapuss – a slave from the Land of the Kitons.
Manager of Spatopia.

Saucus – a soothsayer.
Cursus – a curse carver.
Katrin – a cook.
Cleocatra – a cleaner.
Russell – a crow.
Brutia – a dog. Head of the Imperial bodyguard.

THIS IS THE DIARY OF
SPARTA PUSS

DO NOT READ WHAT IS
RITTEN HERE, OR THE GODESS
WILL TAKE A TERRA BULL
REVENGE ON YOU.

I, CURSUS ROTE THIS

PAWS XVI
March 16th

I AM SPARTAPUSS and this is my diary. I'm new to history but I intend to take pen to paw and write an entry every day after I have made my evening rounds.

As I write, I look out upon Spatopia. It is dark now, so I shall leave the description of my place of work until the light is better. It has been my home for more years than I care to remember. It is said that all cats that bathe have bathed in Spatopia. And quite a few flea-ridden barbarians who have never dipped a paw in water, also come here when our famous 'All you can lick' fish bowls are on the menu.

Here at the spa, we look after all Roman cats. From the humble rat-catcher to the noble senator, from the gladiator to the Spraetorian guard. Everything that I see I shall put down in my diary. I promise to leave no scent unsniffed.

I am not one for gossip but we live in scandalous times, so I fear that a little scandalous writing cannot be avoided. Luckily, I have got hold of a good long scroll, so I'll have plenty of room to get down all the details.

PAWS XVII

March 17th

Why Have a Dog and Bark Yourself?

THIS MORNING my master, Clawdius, was in a strange mood again. He would not come away from his scratching post, even though Katrin cooked him a nice fat dormouse for his breakfast. As I padded past him (going low to the ground, so as not to cause offence), he called me over for a word. He gulped, as if he was coughing up a fur ball. Then he told me that he had been up all night 'going over the accounts'. Last week we sold only five lunches at full price. He ordered me to tell our customers that Spatopia, Rome's Finest Bath and Spa, is famous for its 'legendary lunches'. I speak the truth when I say that the food here is more legionary than legendary. I cannot understand why master Clawdius doesn't leave the running of the spa to me and the rest of his slaves. We know the customers only too well. They don't come because of his connections to the Imperial family. They're only here because we are the only spa south of the river to offer a free powdering and brushing with 'all you can eat' fish bowls. The flea epidemic in the East quarter is still terrible.

Now I must leave my writing and make my way to the kitchen for I smell the spiced chicken roasting and soon it will be in my bowl.

PAWS XVIII

A Foul Deed in the Vomitorium

NOT A GOOD SLEEP last night. A great white goat chased me from dream to dream. I awoke on the floor in a panic. Then, on my morning rounds, I made a terrible discovery. Someone has scrawled a poem on the wall of the vomitorium. I have copied it out. Master Clawdius did not spot it – thank Peus for that! It had been scrawled in plain view, just above the tidemarks from last week's feast.

> *The Emperor Tiberius ruled here in Rome,*
> *Until he went fishing and never came home.*
> *Now Mewlia crouches behind his great throne,*
> *Sniffing and picking away at the bones.*

I rubbed this graffiti off the wall immediately. All poems about the Imperial family were outlawed many years ago by the Emperor Augustpuss, who hated poetry. If this verse was discovered, it would cause a scandal. The writer would wake up one cold night, gazing at the stars, banished to some tiny island at the back end of the Empire.

Master Clawdius could get into the very worst kind of trouble if he were found with that sort of thing on the wall of his vomitorium!

PAWS XIX

March 19th

WILL THE EMPEROR really quit Rome and leave his ancient mother Mewlia on the cushioned throne? I am afraid to write such a thing! There are loose tongues, wandering eyes and thieving paws in this spa. So, to guard this diary's secrets, I have decided to write it in the language of my homeland. For no Roman can speak the language of my homeland, the Land of the Kitons. Romans call Kittish 'the ugliest tongue in the Empire.' If you think that's rude, you should hear what they say about our food.

It has been a very long time since I spoke Kittish. I made the journey from my homeland when I was small, with my eyes only just opened. Tonight I'll remember as much of my native tongue as I can. I've decided to make a list of suspects who may have scrawled the graffiti in the vomitorium. If I write every thing in Kittish, no one will get into trouble if this diary is discovered.

PAWS XX

March 20th

Miaow!

MIOOOW miaooowoo miaaooow miaaooow miaaooow miaaooow miaaooow miaaooow

miaaooow miaaooowo miaaooow miaaooowoo
miaaooow miaaooowoo miaaooow miaaooow-
ooo miaaooow miaaooow miaaooow miaaooow
miaaooowoo miaaooow miaaooow miaaooow
mtaaooowoo miaaooow miaaooow miaaooow
miaaooowoo miaaooow miaaooow...

For Peus sake! Kittish is not a very good language for writing things down! This is going to take an age. I shall just have to risk writing it plainly in Catin as before. But that is enough writing for today, as I can smell fish roasting and soon it will be in my bowl.

PAWS XXI

March 21st

Unusual Suspects

THERE IS STILL NO CLUE as to the identity of the graffiti scrawler. Whoever wrote the rude verses must be someone who dislikes Mewlia, the Emperor's mother. That's a long list, for Peus sake! When it was written, the vomitorium was locked. However, there are a few members of staff who could have got their paws onto a key:

Suspect I: Cursus the curse carver
He is not a likely suspect, because he does not care for politics or poetry. He's not interested in anything apart from gladiators, carving curses and vermin control.

Note: Never get Cursus talking about rats in front of customers! His mouth is as wide as the rolling river Tiber and nearly as filthy.

Suspect II: Saucus the soothsayer
He is a cat of letters and has written poems before, but he's a great defender of the Imperial family and knows better than to write bad things about Clawdius' grandmother.

Suspect III: Russell
A possible suspect. He has strange views on the Imperial family, especially for a crow.

Suspect IV: Katrin the cook
Coming from Purrmania, she can't read or write much Catin, except for the odd recipes. Surely not Katrin?

Suspect V: Cleocatra the cleaner
Not Cleocatra either. She cannot stand graffiti, for she is the one who has to scrub it all off.

Enough! For I hear Clawdius at his scratching post.

PAWS XXII
March 22nd

TODAY CLAWDIUS was being unreasonable. He threw a vase full of cold water at me to rouse me from my cushion. Then he complained about the noise. Apparently, some wild beasts are camping outside our gates. Their howling was particularly bad this afternoon. I told Clawdius that it is no use ordering me to go and evict them, for they are on the other side of our wall. They are on the public road, and so he must call the Spraetorian guard to move them on.

I confess that I'm afraid to approach these beasts as they are bigger than me – and wilder! As for the identity of the graffiti scrawler – I have no more clues as yet, but I am stalking certain members of staff!

PAWS XXIII

March 23rd

The Slyness of the Beasts

THE NOISE from those wild beasts is getting worse. They were making a terrible row this morning. I think they were having an argument about sleeping places. At any rate, they disturbed master Clawdius from his nap. Our customers might make fun of his speech, but there is certainly nothing wrong with his hearing. He ordered me to move his basket to the other side of the courtyard, so as to avoid the dreadful din. Funny that he didn't mention the smell.

More ill news: my diary is supposed to be a secret but already half the spa is congratulating me on my new hobby as a 'cat of letters'. I have had offers of help from a number of customers who want to school me in the art of writing. I have decided to follow the advice of Saucus. He says I must read as little as possible so that my work will not be corrupted with the style of other writers. Saucus gave me another good piece of advice. On no account should I ever think before writing things down, for if thoughts hang around the brain too long they must surely come out rotten. I shall start now with a description of Clawdius, my master.

Clawdius

His fur is grey. It is not as thick as it used to be. He walks with an unusual roll, as if his back legs do not know where his front legs are going. He has walked like this since birth. His speech is strange. Saucus says that he was born at a time when the pawtents were bad and that the gods made him walk and talk like a fool. They did this in order to punish his mother for not honouring them with the right sacrifices. It is true that his was a difficult birth and his own mother was surprised that he lasted past the first week. Katrin says he speaks strangely because he has an exceptionally large tongue, which is too big for his mouth. She says he dribbles all over his pillow at night. She showed me the pillow in question and it was badly stained with drool. But there is nothing wrong with my master's eyes. Today he caught a couple of strays selling our brushes on a stall in the market! And there was no hesitation in his speech when he called the Spraetorian guard to arrest them.

PAWS XXVIII

March 28th

The Scrawler Strikes Again

ILL NEWS. This morning I discovered a new verse, in the same place as before. The writing was even wobblier than the last time, yet strangely familiar.

Mice run the Empire, the Senate are rats,
Mewlia acts like she's Queen of the Cats.

It was signed V.S. which must stand for 'Vomitorium Scrawler'. Luckily Cleocatra the cleaner was passing, so she helped me to scrub it off. Clawdius would climb the city walls if he knew about this!

I doubt that I shall get a good night's sleep. Last night the same terrible goat chased me from dream to dream. I fear I may have eaten too much. I had a lovely dinner of my favourite spiced chicken, which Katrin cooked 'Kitish style' – roasted to blackened perfection.

PAWS XXIX

March 29th

The Bodyguards

THIS AFTERNOON Brutia came charging through the gates accompanied by the Emperor's bodyguards. They were shouting, 'We've come for

Clawdius! We've come for Clawdius!'

I was like a frightened rabbit in front of a pack of hounds. I feared that someone had told them about the Vomitorium Scrawler and they'd come to arrest Clawdius. But Brutia had only come to complain about the noise from the wild beasts.

Brutia is the kind of dog that seizes her problems by the throat and shakes them. I circled her a few times and then tried to explain that Clawdius was busy with important business. I added that there was very little we could do about what goes on outside the spa walls.

She called me a 'Stinking flea-ridden Kiton slave'. That is a lie, I am most particular about my coat. Then she gave me a nasty nip on the tail, and threatened to rip it off for a duster if her evening bath was ever interrupted again.

It is a good thing that I have been trained to agree with the customers as frequently as possible and cross them in nothing. This is wise advice in the case of this customer! She commands the Imperial bodyguards. Most of them are big Purrmanians, captured in the wars in the Neuterberger forest. They are sworn to defend the Emperor with their lives. They're bred for their loyalty, unlike the Spraetorian guards, who'll usually bend the rules for a decent piece of fish.

When she'd gone, Cursus told me it was no use complaining. Apparently Brutia likes arguments, and she always wins! Luckily, Clawdius wasn't around when this was going on. Katrin kindly bandaged my bitten tail and I shall try dipping it in the Sacred Spring if it has not improved by tomorrow morning.

PAWS XXX

March 30th

More Beastly Behaviour

TODAY WE APPROACHED the wild beasts to complain about the noise. Russell agreed to be my interpreter. He speaks many languages and has something of a way with the wild ones.

Russell told me that these wild beasts are good types for the most part, but a little over-enthusiastic sometimes. Their camp has got bigger and the noise they make is considerable. The stench they give off is dreadful. It creeps under the walls and puts customers off their dinners. The bears are the worst offenders, but the wolves and tigers could also do with a wash.

We approached with caution. Russell flew over and got their attention first. He has a marvellous voice for public speaking so I gave him the list of Clawdius' complaints to read out. On hearing these, the wild beasts acted all innocent, claiming that they could not smell anything at all except for crow, cat and the stink of scented rose-water from our side of the wall. They would not listen to reason so I offered them kitchen scraps and a silver coin a night if they could keep the noise down for the rest of the week. We left them disputing how the money should be divided up.

APURILIS I

April 1st

TODAY THE WILD BEASTS were far quieter, thank Mewpiter! Money is the mother of invention! Brutia ought to be glad, or if not actually pleased, at least she should be no more ill-tempered than usual.

APURILIS II

April 2nd

Of Mice and Pen

A MOUSE GAVE ME THE SLIP in the caldarium today. It should have been an easy catch but it got away behind the towel baskets.

Last night I dreamt about the graffiti that we found in the vomitorium. Some would say that the line in the first poem about the emperor who never came home is a pawtent. I have the feeling that something bad is about to happen. There are many here in Spatopia who believe in signs. Clawdius uses soothsayers and he even consults the Moracle every five years. I confess that I have never been impressed with the advice of astrologers. But, just in case, I decided to pay Saucus the soothsayer a visit. I made him swear by Mewpiter that he would not reveal what he was about to hear. But he laughed and told me he'd already heard all about the Scrawler, from one of the customers. For Peus' sake! Some of the tongues in this place could give wagging lessons to the dogs!

Saucus got his book of star charts out and sat staring at a piece of sky above the roof. He says that if you study the stars for long enough, you can recognise their pictures or read messages from the gods. I'm afraid they all look like fiery dots to me. As I was paying him by the hour, I was relieved when a large raven landed on the roof. It would not move, even though it attracted quite a crowd including two Spraetorian guards with slingshots. Saucus interpreted this as a sign that the Emperor Tibbles will not leave Rome for Capri, like the poem predicts.

APURILIS III

April 3rd

A Near Miss

I WAS CROSSING the gymnasium in search of a basket of missing towels when I was almost speared by a stray javelin. It was thrown with such force that I was nearly skewered like a rat kebab. It was not a deliberate plot to take my life. The thrower was a senator who had recently enrolled in one of our beginners' pilum classes and was getting some throwing tips from a friend. I overheard him say that the Emperor Tiberius is definitely planning to retire to the island of Capri. So much for Saucus' predictions! He isn't the most far-sighted astrologer in the capital. His own house has burnt down three times!

I learned that the Emperor Tiberius is in the middle of constructing a luxury villa on the island of Capri, where he loves the fishing. Cursus knows one of the builders and, apparently, the centrepiece is a blue and white mosaic of a bowl of cream, with the inscription 'Lick Me!' picked out in gold tiles.

APURILIS IV

April 4th

THERE ARE WHISPERS all over the spa about the Emperor's trip to Capri. Will he retire for good or is it another holiday? If he retires, who will he appoint as Rome's new ruler? Some say that he will restore the Repurrblic and we'll be ruled by the Senate instead of an emperor. But most here think that Tibbles will pass his throne on to a member of his own family.

Clawdius' brother Purrmanipuss would have made a wonderful emperor. Poor Purrmanipuss. It is the anniversary of his death next week and Clawdius will be in mourning again. No wonder he has been off his food.

APURILIS V

April 5th

I WAS TOO BUSY to worry about pawtents today, as I have to get everything ready. Clawdius is going to visit the Senate tomorrow and he has ordered me to come with him.

APURILIS VI

April 6th

A Trip to the Senate

YESTERDAY AT NOON Clawdius and I walked to the Senate. Or rather, I padded and Clawdius shuffled along behind me, dragging his bad leg through the dirt.

As we passed under the triumphal arch the morning sun was high in the sky. But the golden statue of the Emperor Tiberius wasn't gleaming in the sunlight. It stood cold, in the shadow of the monument to Mewlia. Ever since her statue was erected, it has been said that 'the mother robs her son of his afternoon warmth', which is a little cruel. I wouldn't dare to say anything of that sort in front of Clawdius for he has always respected Mewlia. She is his grandmother, even though they are not close. She treats him like a halfwit.

As we passed the statues, a shaft of light reflected off Mewlia's outstretched paw, casting a beam upon Tibbles' left eye. It was as if Mewlia was stabbing him with a burning spear. Another pawtent perhaps?

When we arrived at the Senate there was a great hissing from the crowds. As a member of the Imperial family, Clawdius deserves respect. But it gives me no pleasure to say that he has never been very popular with the crowds. Exactly why is a mystery to me. Katrin believes that they pick up on his nervousness.

25

When he speaks he mixes up his words, like a neuter or a foreigner. Cursus says that the crowds dislike him because he is too bookish and refuses to exercise, even in his own gymnasium. So I was relieved to find out that no one was hissing at Clawdius. The mob were angry because there was no more free fish to be had at the food stalls, not even a sardine!

We'd only just taken our places in the Senate house when the fanfare sounded. The Emperor and his mother Mewlia entered, accompanied by their Purrmanian bodyguards. Brutia lurked at Caesar's side, as usual. I did my best to blend into the crowd, for my tail still aches from the biting she gave me.

Senator Pusspero rose from the cushion to give the formal greeting to the Emperor. He struggled to make himself heard above the shouts of 'Hail Tibbles! Hail his mighty Tibbs!' from outside the hall.

Tiberius' purple robe and golden cushions matched Mewlia's perfectly. It is said that she still picks out all of her son's outfits for him. She's always had a passion for jewels and her collars are the talk of the capital. This time, she'd outdone herself. She wore a golden ruff, set with sapphires as big as shark's eyes. It fitted her rather tightly around the neck in a style that is currently popular amongst the young.

Mewlia flicked her tail disapprovingly and gazed around the room. Quite what had angered her was impossible to say but it was not hunger, for she had been snacking on portions of raw cod, judging by the smell of it.

Finally, the Emperor Tiberius sprang from his cushion and addressed the hall.

'Right Senators, let's get on with it. We're here for our honours,' he said.

Yowls of horror spread around the hall. With their mind on his retirement, the Senators had completely forgotten the honours that they were supposed to have arranged for the Emperor.

Senator Pusspero spoke next.

'Noble Caesar, forgive us. We were coming to that. But since you bring it up, let us settle it now. Senators, I propose that a new triumphal arch be built at the gates of the Arena in honour of our beloved Emperor Tiberius and Mewlia, who has been like a kindly mother to Rome these many years past.'

Mewlia fixed him with a cold stare.

I fear she may have taken the 'many years' part of his introduction as something of an insult.

There was silence. Then someone added:

'This mighty arch shall of course be decorated with garlands of the highest quality, imported from the land of the Furroahs.'

'Flowers from Fleagypt?' yawned Mewlia.

Then a voice from the back called:

'I propose that in addition to this, two new statues should be built by the triumphal arch at the gates of the Arena itself. Big ones!'

Clawdius flicked his tail and let out a hiss. The

Arena is opposite Spatopia. The last thing we need is a pair of statues overshadowing our gardens.

Again, there was silence. Then someone else added: 'These marvellous statues will be the tallest in Rome!'

Senator Pusspero took up the theme.

'And, of course, to remember the great debt that Rome owes to the Emperor, we will pay for everything. I'm sure that everyone in Rome will want to contribute.'

Clawdius flicked his tail and hissed again.

'And?' asked Mewlia.

'And I hereby propose that, the mighty statues of Caesar and his mother should be made entirely of the finest...'

'Bronze' muttered a voice beside me.

Thankfully, Mewlia didn't hear the remark.

'Speak up Pusspero, you twisted old half-wit!' she demanded. 'What will they be made of?'

'Gold! Let them be made of gold!' replied the old senator, with impressive enthusiasm.

'It is settled then. They will be the tallest and most beautiful statues Rome has ever seen!' added Pusspero.

'And furthermore, I propose that the new statues of our Emperor and his adored mother, be cleaned monthly by a trained craftsman equipped with wiping cloths of the finest leather, a silver ladder and a golden bucket,' suggested someone else.

Mewlia seemed content with this.

'That will do, I suppose. But aren't you forgetting

someone?' she asked, rising from her cushion.

The Senator was puzzled. Tiberius rolled his eyes.

'Someone who has a birthday very soon. Someone who will need to be honoured when he assumes the silver collar at his coming of age.'

There was a pause.

'Catligula! Let's have a statue of young Catligula!' shouted a voice. Brutia ordered a search for the offender. It is well known that Gattus cannot stand the nickname Catligula. It was given to him when he grew up in camp with the legions.

'Catligula, Catligula, he's such a lovely figula!' cheered the crowd outside the hall. News travels fast!

Senator Pusspero spoke once more.

'Noble Mewlia, once again you teach the Senate another valuable lesson by reminding us all of our duty to honour Rome's future as well as its past.' He sounded less nervous than before.

'But what sort of honours should we bestow upon Catlig... I mean the noble Gattus Tiberius?

Mewlia presented him with a scroll, which the senator unfolded and read out:

'We, the Senate, do hereby honour the noble Gattus Tiberius as follows: on the occasion of his tenth birthday, a statue of him, made of solid gold is to be erected in Paws Field by the temple of Mewpiter. Furthermore Gattus shall be guest of honour at the Games of Purrcury to be held at the Arena. These games shall include a Wild Beast Hunt and sacrifices in his honour, at the public expense. Participating beasts are to be genuinely fierce and of a quality that shall provide good entertainment.'

Before Pusspero had finished reading, Mewlia and Tibbles were already making their way out of the hall. Many in the crowd were disappointed, for Tiberius had left before saying anything about his retirement and the Senate, it seems, had thought it best not to ask him directly.

Clawdius was quiet and sullen as we returned to the spa. I fear that the expense of the statues has put him in a bad mood.

APURILIS VII

April 7th

THE WHOLE OF ROME is talking about Catligula. He's very young to have his own statue. A solider, who came in to get his claws clipped, told me that the legions adore Catligula. Apparently, they loved his father Purrmanipuss, the great general. It is said he'll become a famous soldier too. Surely he'll be Tiberius' choice as a successor when he retires?

Saucus says if Catligula becomes Emperor it will suit master Clawdius very nicely. I thought they hated each other. But Saucus is sure that they are the best of friends, because you can always spot them sitting next to each other at the games.

Mewlia has deliberately kept Clawdius away

from public in case he causes an embarrassment. The Emperor Augustpuss gave him a role at the Games once, but that was a disaster. He was distracted by a passing gull and couldn't get his words out right.

APURILIS VIII
April 8th

MY DIARY is not a place for gossip but I have just heard the most extraordinary tale. Cleocatra the cleaner has a sister called Neferkitti who works at the Imperial Palace. She says that yesterday Catligula was seen charging from room to room, brandishing a huge cod he'd taken from the larder. He was thrusting it in the faces of passers by, insisting that it was a sword. Then he said that he, Gattus the Great, was training for the Games of Purrcury. He swore by Hercatules, the god of the gladiators, that he would strike down the next beast to enter the Arena. Even if the beast was fierce and deadly, even if the battle should last a year or more – he didn't care. He asked if anybody wanted to bet that he couldn't conquer any beast that entered. But who should come padding along but his elderly tutor Cato the Younger? Catligula sprang upon the old one and began to strike him with the codfish shouting: 'Surrender beast or die!' As he chased poor Cato all about the palace, a sizeable crowd followed behind. At last he cornered the old one in the laundry, where he'd taken refuge in a washing basket. Catligula pretended that he didn't know where Cato was hiding for a moment, but then he got the bodyguards to empty out all the baskets. Poor old Cato tumbled out with a load of dirty towels.

Apparently Catligula would not cease his attack until the old tutor rolled over onto his back and waved his legs in the air in submission.

I do not know if this story is true but I expect it will be all around the spa by noon, if I know Cleocatra.

APURILIS IX
April 9th

TODAY THEY set the date for the wild beast hunt in honour of Catligula's birthday. It is to be held at the Games of Purrcury. Russell flew over to the beasts' camp to warn them about the danger they are in. The bears, being sceptical creatures by nature, did not believe him until he showed them this poster.

GAMES OF PURRCURY
Featuring...
Gladiators
Wild Beast Hunt
... and lots more Violent Sport!

Please bring your own cushions, as the seats in the Arena are hard.

The poster showed two beast fighters. The first had a

rectangular shield and a gladius, like they use in the legions. The second fighter had a net and a trident. Its three prongs were pointed at the neck of a chained bear. In the corner, wild animals were cowering in fear as a crowd cheered on the two bestiari.

Although the animals on the poster were badly drawn, the wild beasts didn't take much convincing. They did not want to get rounded up and herded into the Arena. We watched as they left one by one, leaving only a cloud of dust and a frightened smell in the air.

APURILIS X
April 10th

LAST NIGHT I SLEPT SOUNDLY. The wild beasts are gone. I know that I have complained about them before in this diary, but I almost miss them now. I suppose we should be thankful they have escaped to safety, and grateful for the peace and quiet. At least Brutia won't drown me in the cold plunge pool now.

APURILIS XII
April 12th

THIS MORNING more customers were complaining about the noise. For a moment I thought that the wild beasts had returned – but it is the row from the workers who have started building the Imperial statues in time for the games. I told the complainers that the civilised world eagerly awaits the invention of the silent hammer. This shut them up for a bit.

Talking of buildings, I am told that carving the new statue of the Emperor is causing a most vexing problem for the craftsmen. Should it be carved with a double chin, as in real life?

APURILIS XIV

April 14th

A Very Important Visit

NEWS OF GREAT IMPORTANCE! In just five days we are to be honoured with a visit from the Emperor Tiberius himself! He is to stop here at Spatopia for lunch on his way to the island of Capri. The official word is that he is off on his annual fishing holiday. But the rumours of his retirement continue.

Clawdius is taking a personal interest in the visit and he is determined that everything is to be done correctly, following all the rules, and that all the proper ceremonies are to be observed. He told me that he does not want to come out of it 'looking like I've got fur for brains,' like last time. It is true that there have been some problems with previous Imperial visits to the spa. Who could have predicted that a stuck valve in the caldarium would have led to an explosive blowback through the ceremonial fountain?

Besides, Clawdius made a tidy sum by renting extra towels that day, and hot mud on the pads has since become a popular beauty treatment for females.

Clawdius has ordered us to practise. We will have a full rehearsal on the day before the visit. I have assured my master that all will go well. He'll be proud of the staff of Spatopia, who will 'operate with the precision of a machine,' as they say in the legions. I have read in that a good team, working together can perform better than any one individual – however hard-working that one cat might be. This is surely true of our team here at the spa. For the day of the visit at least, we shall be Rome's Finest Bath and Sacred Spa.

APURILIS XV

April 15th

PREPARATIONS FOR THE EMPEROR'S VISIT are well under way. Well, they are under way! Concerning the food, Master Clawdius told Katrin that he has never tasted duller food than the refreshments that she served today. He said that the food was not fit to grace the table of a drainage engineer, let alone the table of the Emperor of the civilised world. This was probably not the best example he could have chosen, since Katrin's first husband, Drusus, was a drainage engineer. I have asked her to see if she can come up with some new recipes that are more suitable to the Imperial palate, with a bit of spice to them.

I have made a full list of tasks for the staff of Spatopia:

I Cleocatra

Scrub the main bathing pool thoroughly and rinse down after cleaning. Do not use any cleaning product that will damage the tiles.

II Katrin

Make a sacrifice to the mighty Neptuna so that all will go well in the kitchen.

III Russell

Fly around and inspect all surfaces for cleanliness. Do not perch on the vomitorium roof as this may confuse Saucus' astrological predictions.

IV Saucus

Please refrain from predicting future events that may cause offence to the Emperor or his guests.

V Cursus

Keep customers' carvings clean and to the point. Carve backwards where possible.

APURILIS XVII

April 17th

Two Days to the Imperial Visit

THE CLEANING CONTINUES and Katrin is working on the new menu. She has had a word with one of her contacts over at the Imperial kitchen, to see if he can find out what the Emperor's favourite dishes may be. Any small details could give us an advantage.

The pool by the Sacred Spring was drained today and it was full of curses carved onto pewter plates. I suppose that it must have been hard for Cursus to resist carving, as he earns a silver denarius per curse. But he has disobeyed my orders. I shall have to speak to him after the visit.

APURILIS XVIII

April 18th

One Day to the Imperial Visit

WHAT A DAY OF DISASTERS. Chaos has kicked Mewpiter from his cushion at the top of Mount Olympuss! I found an algal bloom in the caldarium, a leak in the overflow pipe and someone has done something unspeakable in the main bathing pool, turning the water yellow.

It is lucky that master Clawdius is a student of the stroic philosophy, whose followers are famous for mastering their feelings and keeping their tempers under control. As for the food, Katrin has been experimenting to find out what holds its flavour best when baked inside a swan – the dormouse or the vole.

Clawdius was not impressed with either sample calling it 'A meal unfit for a road builder, let alone the Emperor himself,'

He could have picked his words better since Katrin's second husband was a road builder from Purrsia.

However, there is some good news about the menus. Katrin's contact at the palace kitchen tells us that oysters are the Emperor Tiberius' favourite food. They are quite the thing in the Imperial court nowadays and Cursus is friendly with a fish seller who has oysters in plentiful supply. If Fortune is with us, even after this day's disasters, we can hope for a feast tomorrow that will be fit for an emperor. But now, if I am not mistaken, I can smell the spiced chicken roasting and there is just time for a bowl before I take to my basket.

MAIUS V

May 5th

Oh Gods! What Have I Done?

IT IS ONLY NOW that I can record what has become of me. Now I look back on my times at the spa as a pleasant dream, half faded, that most likely will never be dreamed again. I used to be free from care and I had no worries, except perhaps missing towels or missing takings from the till or concerns about how best to direct the work of the employees of Spatopia. Indeed Master Clawdius used to say that I lived a charmed life. It seems charmless now. What a world is this, where life and death are ruled by the most trivial of events, a few words said or left unsaid, a chance event that comes to pass. Do the gods plan this for us, or do they look down and laugh? Now I know why they speak of the goddess Fortune as a spinner. The fruits of her labour are delicate threads of fate and I am living proof that they can snap at any time. Now I lie caged in a cell, entertaining only loneliness, with nothing to look forward to but a violent death. Though I shall never make sense of it, I shall set it down in this diary so that history will know exactly what became of poor Spartapuss.

We were preparing for the visit of the Emperor Tiberius. All had been made ready after that disastrous dress rehearsal the previous day. The staff worked hard all through the night. At dawn, Cursus came with me to the fish market to help me buy the oysters. His contact there was a fellow named Carpus, who swore he could do us a good deal. He swore a lot as I recall.

In the temple, Saucus lit the sacrificial fires. Katrin laid out the feast on low tables.

We'd planned everything. Music was provided by a group that Russell had hired especially for the event. Hissiod was on lyre, Catia on pipes and Maxipuss on percussion. They wanted three denari each but I haggled them down to a silver coin between them and as much of the oyster buffet as they could eat.

The customers were getting excited, having arrived early to find a spot with a good view of the Emperor.

The spa was packed with regulars and I also spotted some new faces and strays who'd come especially for the visit. Clawdius had given us strict instructions to charge the newcomers double to get in and to make sure we sold plenty of souvenir drinking bowls.

As the hour of the visit approached, I was still busy with last-minute checks. Shortly before Tiberius was due to arrive we received a visit from Brutia, with the Imperial body guards loping along obediently behind her as usual. I felt a twinge go through my tail as she passed. Then the musicians struck up with a familiar tune called *Hush! Caesar Best and Greatest Approaches*.

Clawdius greeted Brutia but struggled to get his words out, choking as if upon a fur ball. Eventually he managed:

'Greetings Brutia, defender of Rome. We are honoured that the Emperor Tiberius should choose to visit our simple but recently redecorated spa...'

'Save your breath,' said Brutia. 'The Emperor's not coming. He's gone to Capri. After the sharks.'

The guests were naturally very disappointed to hear that the visit was cancelled. There was uproar amongst the crowd and shouts of 'We want Tibbles!' and 'Refund! Refund!' When the band realised what was happening, they struck up with a sad song entitled *Oh News of Great Disappointment*.

I couldn't help but think of the care and effort that had gone into the preparations for the Emperor's visit. All our hard work would be for nothing. If Clawdius was disappointed, he managed to hide it well.

'How unexpected! Perhaps Tiberius may honour us with a visit some other time. We are, as ever, at the service of the Emperor and the whole Imperial family.'

'Good' said Brutia, 'because Gattus is visiting you instead. He's been delayed by the crowds, but he'll be here any moment.'

When Clawdius heard that Gattus – 'Catligula' – was coming instead of the Emperor, he went as pale as his marble floor.

Clawdius gave us clear instructions. He warned us not to use the nickname Catligula, we must be sure to refer to our guest by his proper name Gattus. (I shall go on writing with the nickname Catligula for they cannot put me to death twice.) Clawdius also warned us not to speak to Catligula unless he asked us a direct question and never to look him directly in the eyes. In a low voice, Clawdius whispered what we knew already, that on no account should anyone mention the word 'goat' in Catligula's presence or look him in the eyes as he was easily provoked by a stare.

It is said that Catligula hates goats more than any creature because he was cruelly butted in the Imperial gardens when he was young. But it is whispered that he dislikes them so much because he has something of a goatish look about him

Outside, the band had struck up with the popu-lar tune *Miaow if You Love Catligula!* (to which the unofficial chorus goes 'Hiss and he'll skin you alive').

Through the gates came an enormous green chair

carried by four attendants. On a pile of golden cushions sat Catligula. His friend Liccus, the famous actor, was seated opposite. Brutia and the Imperial bodyguards snarled at the crowd to keep them back.

'My dear G-G-Gattus, what an unexpected surprise! You honour us here with your presence,' said Clawdius.

'Uncle Claw you old tomcat, I bet you've got some wild surprise for me, haven't you? It's my birthday next week and I love surprises. Racing chariots would be amusing. Or gladiators in a pitched battle? Or a wild beast hunt with me on an elephant at the front? What would you suggest Liccus?'

Liccus answered without hesitation:

'Let us hold a theatrical spectacular featuring you, Rome's most radiant star, in the most important role.'

'My dear nephew, the facilities of Spatopia are at your disposal, and your guests are all most welcome,' said Clawdius without faltering this time.

'But first, what news of our beloved Emperor? I trust that he is well.'

'That old bruiser? He can't wait to get down to Capri and get after the sharks. What he sees in those brutish fish is quite beyond me. When I'm emperor, I'll dredge them out of the seas and have their silly mouths packed with lead and sewn up tight. Then we'll see if they dare to offend my line with their bites.'

'A fitting punishment for a fish so unworthy of the table,' added Clawdius with a little splutter.

'And talking of the table, you must be tired from your journey. Will you take some refreshments now?'

'Fun first and food later,' said Catligula, 'Let's get on with it – bring on the entertainment. I'll conquer first and work up my appetite – Liccus where have you put my golden bow? I shall take my position behind that waterfall. Sound the tuba, send in the wild beasts and I shall slay them each in turn. The biggest first.'

'Dearest nephew, this is but a simple spa. The waterfall you speak of is our Spring, sacred to the great goddess. There are no wild beasts here – unless you count Mogrippa my first wife's mother.'

'Then bring out the old bruiser and let's have some sport with her,' said Catligula.

On hearing this Master Clawdius began to laugh as if it was the funniest joke that had ever been told in Rome's history.

Russell and I joined in with the laughter but many of the guests seemed reluctant to laugh until there was a clear signal that it was safe.

Catligula acknowledged the joke as his own with a wave of the paw. The crowd began to laugh louder. Then he called Brutia to his side.

'My silly uncle has forgotten the entertainment. Go and round up some wild beasts for hunting.'

Russell flapped for a moment and forgetting Clawdius' advice, stared at Catligula as if he was a worm in the ground. For a Roman he has an unusual distaste for blood sports. Luckily, Catligula was busy telling Brutia about the preparations.

'I will have my hunting tower over there by the waterfall, and mind that you make these beasts fiercer than last time, for I want a proper bloodbath and not another of your silly play fights with tame bears and drugged lions!'

Brutia went off to arrange the entertainment, taking a cohort of bodyguards with her. The guards were equipped with nets, whips and a wooden cage on wheels.

When they had gone, Katrin signalled that the feast was prepared. Clawdius took this opportunity to move us through to the main bathing pool. The banquet had been set out around the edges of the pool on wooden tables. There was roast chicken, fresh fish and a huge supply of oysters. True to his word, Cursus' contact at the fish market had come through for us. You've never seen such a quantity or size of shellfish. The slaves, including Cursus, were already passing round the warmed cream.

As usual, instructions had been given to the servers to save the good stuff for the guests of honour. Catligula was to be served by Katrin herself, who would pass the food to his taster.

Worried that there was no space on the tables for dessert – a trough of cream flavoured with fish oil – Katrin told Cursus to pass round the oysters to clear some space. Catligula's narrow eyes lit up at the sight of the great trays of fishy treats. He let out a little mew of delight.

'Mmmm. These are enormous. Clawdius – where in Neptuna's name did you find them?'

We watched in amazement as he tore into shell after shell and sucked out the slimy contents with his rough tongue.

Unaccustomed to table manners like this, Clawdius hesitated for a moment.

'The c-c-cook can tell us where they are from Nephew. Probably from the Atlantic.'

'Begging your pardon your Imperial Highnesses,' interrupted Cursus, 'This stallholder friend of mine sold us these beauties. And he swears that they come from the cold seas near the island of the Kitons, just a day's sail away from the Land of the Dead. The water there is thickest with the filth that oysters love to feed on. They are bottom feeders you see ...'

'Take my tray slave,' said Clawdius, wanting to stop this talk of filthy filter feeders in its tracks before it put his guest off his lunch.

But Catligula had already stopped stuffing his face with oysters. Now his head was thrown back at a most awkward angle. White and yellow foam bubbled from the sides of his mouth and ran down all over his beautiful shiny coat. His eyes were as narrow as slits and great dribbles of foaming drool ran down his chest and paws.

'I... feel... sick,' he spluttered.

'Fear not, we'll just escort you to the vomitorium

dear nephew,' said Clawdius ordering me to come forward to help.

On seeing this, Liccus and some of the court guests also began to sneer at the shellfish they had been happily scoffing moments before. Some of them started to show symptoms of being violently ill, clutching their stomachs whilst rolling their eyes towards the skies and mewing pitifully. Their illnesses were dramatic but no one was foaming at the mouth like Catligula. Indeed, I have never seen such a bad reaction to food – unless it was the time that Katrin put hard-boiled pike on the menu three nights in a row.

As we helped Catligula up, my heart sank. I knew that Fortune had spun us a wrong one. Then a terrible thought came to mind.

Only seconds after this thought left my mind, the contents of Catligula's meal left his stomach. It broke like a fishy wave against the marble, giving his front paws a light coating in the process. But to my horror, written on the back wall of the vomitorium, in letters clear for all to see was this verse:

> Catligula's statue is beautifully carved,
> So life-like from tail to the throat,
> Except for a paw which is slightly too large,
> And the face like a dirty great GOAT.

'Uncle, what is the meaning of this?' hissed Catligula. 'First you feed me poison. Then you insult me with these... these monstrous verses.'

'The criminal who wrote this filth will be caught and forced to lick it off the wall till his tongue bleeds,' said Clawdius.

This was harsh punishment indeed considering the state of the wall, which Catligula had given a good coating earlier. With a great effort of will, Clawdius gathered his composure. He moved close to Catligula and lowered his voice to a whisper.

'This foaming at the mouth, are you sure it is the food?'

Catligula said nothing. When he threw a temper tantrum his audience usually grovelled, or begged, or rolled around on the floor in submission. But Clawdius, who all in Rome call a fool, remained calm.

'Look around you. No one else foams at the mouth. They ate the same oysters as you. This foam has been sent from the gods. It is a sign of your g-g-greatness!'

'Sometimes I feel, different, as if the gods have great plans for me,' he confessed.

'It is surely a pawtent. Did not the mighty Mewlius Caesar suffer from such attacks?' said Clawdius.

'Mention this to no one,' said Catligula. His anger had dried up, as if someone had turned off a tap.

After I'd cleaned his face, he rose and left the vomitorium. Clawdius and I followed close behind.

Now he prowled towards Brutia who had returned with the guards, from her mission to procure wild beasts. I wondered what poor creature they'd dragged out of its lair for this 'sport'. But the cage was empty.

'Forgive us your Imperial Highness, but there's not a beast to be had in all of Rome,' said Brutia.

Catligula's expression was blank but his tail was flicking.

'What do you mean?' he asked.

'Our informers tell us that they found out about the wild beast hunt at the Games of Purrcury. So they ran away,' said Brutia.

'They may run from your greatness, but they will not get far,' said Liccus nervously.

Caligula looked at him as if he was considering some terrible punishment, like having him drowned in a vat of oysters or walled up in a vault with a sack of rats.

Instead he turned to Clawdius.

'Who is responsible for the food here?' he demanded. Catligula glared around the crowd but no one dared to meet his gaze.

'Speak, mice! Or I will draw your tongues with your own claws,' snapped Brutia.

Then a voice said, 'I know the name of the cook here. She's awful. She deserves to drown in one of her own stews. Her name is Ka...'

But the voice was muffled by an outstretched paw.

'Speak up!' said Brutia.

'The one in ch-charge here is Spartapuss,' said a familiar voice. It was Clawdius.

'Where is the villain hiding?' said Catligula.

'Spartapuss! Make yourself known!' ordered

Brutia, sniffing the air for my scent.

'Spar-ta-puss! Spar-ta-puss!' came a shout from the crowd. Soon others took up the chant.

I wanted to speak. To make some apology, but in all the noise and confusion it was as if another cat had got my tongue. I slipped down behind a column, paws over my ears. Nearby, I heard a shout.

'There he is. He's Spartapuss!'

'No I'm not, I'm Cursus,' said Cursus.

'Spar-ta-puss! Spar-ta-puss!' hissed the crowd.

'For Peus' sake! Never mind, take that old one anyway, he'll do,' said Catligula.

'Into the cage. Now!' barked Brutia. Cursus trembled like a kitten down a well.

'Stop! Wait. It's me. I'm Spartapuss,' I said. 'And I am very sorry. It is all my fault. About the food,' I added.

I dared a quick glance at Clawdius but he said nothing.

'Into the cage. Now!' commanded Brutia.

'We'll need to find him an opponent for our games,' said Catligula.

'Let him fight the old one. I saw him serving the oysters before, if you can call that service,' said Liccus.

'Let Cursus go. I'm responsible for everything,' I pleaded.

Finally Clawdius spoke.

'He's not responsible for everything. What about the publicity? Every wild beast in Rome ran away when they saw the posters. Now who was in charge of that, I wonder?'

Liccus' tongue went white as watered milk.

'Yes uncle! In Paws' name, whoever the fool may be must pay with his blood, wouldn't you agree Liccus?'

Catligula was playing with Liccus now. Both of them knew that the posters had been Liccus' idea. Poor Liccus threw himself to the ground and begged for his life. It had been a mistake. Couldn't one slip be forgotten? When there were no more words of sense, just cries coming from him, Catligula said softly.

'Hush Liccus, all is not lost. Do me one good service and you may win my favour once more.'

'Name it. Anything!' said Liccus, his eyes lit with a little flicker of hope.

'The noblest thing of course, would be to take your own life,' said Catligula, throwing him a dagger.

Liccus looked at the knife. He didn't think his mistake with the posters was worth dying for.

'But your other chance is this. You will fight this wretched poisoner, Spartapuss, in single combat, to the death. Not in the Arena, but here before me now. Wait! Better still, make it over there so I may view it from a shaded spot. If you win, I will let you live,' said Catligula, 'but only if the fight is entertaining.'

Liccus stared at me wide-mawed. I am no fighter but I stood still and met his eyes with a steady gaze. I knew that the only way out of this was to pretend to be brave. So I drew myself up to my full height and unsheathed my claws.

'Ooh! A six claw!' said a voice in the crowd, remarking on the unusual trait in my family that we have six claws on each front paw. Not that this would do me much good, as my claws are kept clipped so short that they could not tear butter. But in his terror Liccus could not see this. He began to back away.

Smelling the fear, the crowd began to hiss. A chant began, 'Spar-ta-puss, Spar-ta-puss, six claw, six claw!'

It wasn't the same chant as before. Then, they were spitting my name out like a diseased mouse. Crowds of this type seem to know by instinct when they're onto a winner, and now they were cheering me as their champion. Not that I had to prove my courage in combat. I took a single step towards poor Liccus and he dropped the dagger, turning to Catligula to plead for his life. He wasn't wild – he could not fight. Was there any other way to serve the great Catligula?

Brutia didn't wait for a command from her master. As soon as Liccus dropped his weapon she lunged towards him, making at least one good contact with her teeth that drew blood. He was overpowered by the guards and thrown into the cage.

I should have thanked Hercatules, the god of the gladiators, for my incredible victory, but I was stunned. Fortune's wheel had turned and rolled my whole world over. But Catligula had not forgotten my offence. Before I could celebrate, Brutia turned towards me and snarled.

'You. Get in the cage. Now!' came the command.

But that is enough writing for now, I hear the guard coming to lock us up tight for the night.

MAIUS VI

May 6th

NOT MUCH SLEEP last night. I can think of nothing but real food. I pray for anything tasty, anything but black rat soup again.

MAIUS VII

May 7th

'Death with Extras'

MY PRAYERS HAVE been granted. The black rat soup was served cold today, and it thickened by itself into a stew. It was served by a mangy gaoler, a ginger like me, who told me to cheer up because the sentence for poisoning is a lifetime of hard labour. Then he said that he was only having a jest with me. The sentence for poisoning is death. It's not surprising really, seeing as the sentence for stealing a grape from the Imperial vines, or an olive from an Imperial tree, is death. He seemed upset that in all the years of the Empire, all the wise heads at our noble Senate hadn't managed to come up with anything worse than death. Something called 'Death with Extras' is what he, and all the other gaolers, would like to introduce. I could tell that he wanted me to ask what the 'extras' were, and when I denied him that pleasure, his tail started flicking and he left in a huff. But not before giving me a piece of his mind. He could give even Cursus a run in a swearing contest. I should consider myself fortunate that I was not executed on the spot, was the gist of it. His parting words to me were: 'If you have friends with money or influence – send word to them now.'

I'm sure that the gaolers make a tidy profit out of allowing visits and messages and so forth. But he won't be making any money from this prisoner. I was taught from the litter that begging is a bad business, and I don't intend to start now.

MAIUS VIII

May 8th

Cold Mouse Mash

M Y SLEEP WAS little better last night. No visitors today, just the ginger gaoler again. When I enquired about the menu, he promised me a change from black rat soup-stew. Today he pushed a plate of cold mouse mash under the door. I was so hungry that I made short work of it. The smell brought back memories of the vomitorium on a summer's day. Even compared to Katrin's experimental dishes, the taste was rancid. To take my mind off this, as I write now I try to remember some important things that I have learned from my life, pieces of information that I would like to pass down the ages. For though I am not a neuter, I have no heirs and nothing to pass on. I have decided to make a list of my important thoughts before it is too late.

I cannot think of anything suitable except a line from one of those 'inspirational mosaics' which we had done in the gymnasium to help the guests do better at their sports. My favourite message was:

You know not what may come to pass, So
live each day as if your last.

But now I think of it, it's not that inspiring if you're in prison awaiting execution. There's nothing to do except dream of afters, or the afterlife.

MAIUS IX

May 9th

MOUSE MASH AGAIN today and it tasted no better than yesterday's. It sets like concrete as the hours pass. I cannot stop thinking of the gaoler's words yesterday. Has anyone tried to send word to me here? Has the message been intercepted? I should put aside all hopes of rescue, as the mangy guard says, the walls here are hope-proofed. No one gets out of here alive without a pardon from the Emperor himself.

MAIUS X

May 10th

WHEN THE GAOLER entered with my meal today his manner was strange. He asked if I had enjoyed yesterday's mouse mash and when I answered him honestly, he said that he hoped I'd find this meal more to my taste. I could not believe it when I found the following letter under a pile of mash:

Dearest Spartapuss,

It is your Katrin writing this note. We are all very sorry for the terrible trouble that you have got into because of the oysters (which Carpus still swears were fresh) and also the graffiti in the vomitorium.

Some customers have had a collection for your gravestone and say that we must have a message engraved upon it saying:
'HERE LIES THE NOBLEST SPA MANAGER OF THEM ALL.'
Others think we should say:
'HERE LIES THE STUPIDEST SPA MANAGER OF THEM ALL.'
The customers are also talking about your fight with Liccus. Some wonder if you could have taken Liccus had he defended his territory, and not dropped his weapon

and turned tail like a frightened kitten.

Cursus sends word that he has received an offer from a promoter to arrange a rematch in the spa gym, in the event that you are not already put to death for poisoning. He has offered an advance in gold, to be paid to your heirs if you die.

Getting an Imperial pardon for such a serious charge will not be easy. But fear not. Saucus says the signs are good and that you are to live a long and eventful life. I'm not sure if that will comfort you, but you should also know that, even now, a friend in high places is working to get you out.

I must go now, as the fish liquor will spoil if it boils for longer than an hour.

P.S.
You must eat this letter to keep it secret so I have written it in squid ink on rice paper.

MAIUS XI

May 11th

A Friend in High Places

HOW KIND of Katrin to send me that letter. It is the tastiest thing that I have eaten since I first set paw in this accursed rat hole. I could hardly sleep for thinking of her words that a friend in high places was 'working' to get me out. Could it be that dear Master Clawdius has not abandoned me and even now is using his influence to secure my safety? As a member of the Imperial family, he must have some influence with the Senate. I know he will not fail me.

MAIUS XII

May 12th

AS I WRITE, I await the return of the mangy gaoler. My hopes soar like Purrcury's fiery chariot (which I have never actually seen but it is supposed to be impressive). I can hardly contain my excitement and I would dance around the cell if it were permitted. With what seemed to be a wink, he told me that I was to prepare to be moved this evening and that it would be to a roomier cell than this, where I should be able to stretch my legs for a while. Can it be that, even now, Master Clawdius is working to free me? I can think of no other explanation, as it is unheard of for prisoners to be moved to a better cell.

MAIUS XIII

May 13th

This Is the End

I WAS MOVED down the corridor to the death cell late yesterday evening. As the mangy gaoler hinted, there is indeed more space and a choice of final meal.

Sadly it is a toss up between the brown mouse stew-soup and the black rat stew-soup. I don't think I shall eat much of either, but apparently the chef will be offended if I made no choice, so mouse it shall be.

This is the end.
Has it really come to this?
Yes.

So I am now prepared for whatever the gods may throw at me. Saucus said that I would live a long and varied life. This is not the first time that his predictions have proved inaccurate. If I am granted entrance to the afterlife, then I may find some way to return as a spirit and take the matter up with him.

I cannot sleep. I hope to be able to come up with some profound thoughts before I quit this world and so I am turning, rather late in the day, to poetry. I got as far as:

Fortune pulled the plug out from the bath of my poor life,
If only I could fill it up, but my taps are running dry.
So when my lifetime's waters have run off down the drain,
Will someone scrub the tidemarks off – and fill it up again?

MAIUS XIV

May 14th

A Lucky Spin from Fortune's Wheel

I AM NOT GOING TO BE EXECUTED. This is due to a sudden and unexpected change in the law. The guards were more amazed than I was. A poster in the corridor explains it:

> *By order of the great Emperor Tiberius, all prisoners are invited to participate in the games held in celebration of Gattus Tiberius' birthday. Those prisoners who do not wish to participate in the games should make themselves known to a guard immediately.*

Under this main message was written:

> *Imperial doctor's warning: refusing to participate in the games will result in certain painful death.*

So I'm back in my original cell. I used to think it was a cramped rat hole! I never thought I'd be glad to see it again – or pleased that mouse and rat soup-stews are back on the menu. And another good spin from Fortune, for it has turned out well that I didn't insult the chef by refusing my last meal yesterday.

MAIUS XV

May 15th

News from the Spa

THE GINGER GUARD brought me another note from Katrin. It reads as follows:

Dearest Spartapuss,

We heard reports that you had been moved to the death cell and then moved back. 'Aren't you the lucky one!' says Cursus. Word from Cleocatra's sister at the palace is that you have Mewlia to thank for this. When she saw the catering bill from the prison kitchen, she was furious that the criminals on death row cost so much to feed. I suppose you do eat a lot, what with last meals and so on. And she was also angry that gladiators demand extra pay for fighting to the death. So she has solved both problems with one law. Prisoners must now fight to the death in the Arena at the next games. This reminds me of words of wisdom about problem solving from the Spatopia training manual about putting two problems together to make a solution. You told us all to learn it off by heart. I cannot recall it now, but no matter,

I am sure that you can remember it and it is bringing you comfort.

Since your arrest things have taken a bad turn, and we go to the Sacred Spring every day and pray that the goddess may do something about the one who looks like a goat. Do you know who I mean? I cannot write his name on paper but, to give you a clue, his new golden statue has already become a bird-magnet. Golden bucket or no, it'll take oceans of lime juice to clean the mess off.

Mewlia has bullied the Senate into introducing a new law. To make up for the shortage of wild beasts for Catligula's birthday games, any animal that cannot produce a pedigree certificate shall be declared 'wild'. Wild animals may be rounded up at any time. Most of us don't have pedigree certificates and everyone is suspicious of everyone else. We pray for your release every day. Remember, your friend in high places has not forgotten you.

P.S.
Cursus asks if you have given any thought to a rematch with Liccus, as the promoter is still keen. He suggests 'The Alarum in the Forum' as a good name for it.

MAIUS XVI

May 16th

A Cruel Law

MY DREAMS were wild last night, flitting about like startled starlings. I can think of nothing but the new No-Pedigree law.

I cannot believe that the Emperor agrees to it and no senator dares to speak against it. Few in Rome have a pedigree that proves they come from pure stock. Will those who cannot find enough bribe money be dragged to the Arena for Catligula's entertainment?

MAIUS XVII

May 17th

A Trip in the Night

IWAS WOKEN before first light with the poke from a sharp stick and given a few moments to collect my things. I was not excited this time, as I wanted to avoid another disappointment. The mangy gaoler and a big ginger herded me into a cage. The ginger had fish breath from last night. I was told: 'You are going on a nice little trip. Do not try anything or we will nip your ears off.'

Cloths were placed over the cage but I peeked out and got a good view of the route. It was no more than an hour's journey. I almost cried as we passed Spatopia. Pea green and purple flags were flying outside the Arena in honour of Catligula, for the forthcoming Games of Purrcury. We passed the Arena and went on for a couple of streets before drawing up at the side gate of a building with high walls. The guards exchanged words and I could smell roasting sardines on the fire – they smelled better than the fish on ginger's breath. We were bundled out into the courtyard and then marched to our cells. There are many prisoners here, I can tell by their scents. I pray to the gods that help from high places will come soon. They can only mean to fight us to the death.

MAIUS XVIII

May 18th

My First Day at School

I AM SETTLING IN HERE as well as can be expected. My new cell has a scratching post and I'm to be allowed into the canteen for meals with the other prisoners. Some of them look a bit feral, so I have decided to keep low to the ground and avoid eye contact. Prisoners can be very territorial. Today I was issued with a collar and tag. We are to be trained to fight, they say, because although we are worthless as prisoners, rich patrons will always pay good money to see a gladiator die well.

MAIUS XIX

May 19th

TODAY THE GUARDS put up a poster. They are going to fight us to the death in this order:

I.   Murderers of Imperial family members
II.   Clowns and street entertainers
III. Burglars and thieves
IV.   Plotters and poisoners
V.   Anyone the Emperor dislikes
VI.   Deserters and runaway slaves
VII. Spies and suspicious strays
VIII. Non-pedigrees and anyone with odd looking markings

To ensure that good sport is given on the day of the games, training will be provided.

Next to this there was another poster that was attracting a lot of interest:

Receive personal training from Doctors in the Arts of Combat

Making an end of it
You only die once, so do it well!
Learn to die like a pro.
Doctor: Dogren of Purrmania
Meet at the forge at noon.

Win the Crowd and Win Your Freedom
Old tricks from a pro who knows the fight
game. (Now retired after over a hundred
victorious appearances.)
Doctor: Bogan the Trayjan
Meet at the armoury at first light.

The Art of Unharmed Combat
Doctor: Tefnut

I studied these until a guard gave me a hard poke in
the ribs with the shaft of his spear and shouted:
'Get a move on mousy, we'll have no slacking in this
family, father's orders. It's a good job we're low on
coals otherwise you'd be a case for the hot pokers.'

I wasn't sure what he was talking about, or what his
father had to do with anything. But I didn't like the
sound of hot pokers. I later found out that 'the Father'
is the name for the owner of this gladiatorial school.
And here in the ludus, under his roof, the Father's
word is law.

The guards herded us into the canteen for dinner.
We newcomers were still shackled together by means
of chains between our spiked collars. It was chaos.
Cats were not born to be herded, or chained together
and getting them to walk in pairs is almost impossible.
With much straining and nipping at the back paws
of the prisoner in front, we made it to the canteen.
Dinner was soup, some grass to aid the digestion, and
a main course of roasted chicken. I almost purred

myself unconscious when I saw the chicken, and that it was not a trick, and that everyone else was tearing into theirs. It was the most delicious thing I have ever tasted. Apparently the food in here is carefully prepared to help with our training. You can't fight on an empty stomach and an extra layer of fat protects against blows in combat. The only thing that let this glorious feast down was the dessert. It was rat pudding with raisins. At least I think they were raisins.

Our training starts tomorrow.

A SECOND ENTRY in my diary today. I awoke from a doze to a rattle at the cell door.

'Who's there?' I called out.

'A visitor,' came the reply from the first guard.

'For you!' added a second guard rather unnecessarily. He wasn't the sharpest cat of his litter.

My heart leapt. Maybe Fortune's wheel had turned: first the chicken dinner and now a visitor. For a moment, I dared to hope that it could be a friend. Was Clawdius coming to my aid?

'A new addition to our family,' said the guard.

'But be careful mousy, as she's liable to bite,' added his friend.

The two of them heaved a blanketed bundle through the door. The bundle was tied with leather cord. A third guard stepped in, drew out a long knife, and cut the cord. Then he retreated, slamming the cell door behind him in a hurry. I caught a familiar scent but it was neither friend nor feline. Brutia was cowering low to the ground in the corner of my cell, under a dirty blanket. As I write, she sleeps lightly, twitching as she chases some unfortunate animal through her dreams. I dare not go on with my writing for too long in case she wakes up.

MAIUS XX

May 20th

The No-Peds

BRUTIA IS ASLEEP AGAIN. She sleeps whenever she gets the chance: perhaps she has lost her taste for the waking world. It is said that when a dog is betrayed by its master it loses first its bite, then its bark, and then it dies of a broken heart.

Brutia has not exactly told me her story, but I am piecing it together from what she says in her sleep. In her dreams she continues to fight old battles.

From what I can gather, her patrols searched the city by day and night, hunting for those without the proper pedigree papers. No-Peds were arrested, fined and ordered to return with their documents. But papers were impossible to get. So they would be followed and picked up again. There was no evading Brutia's crew when they had your scent. When there was not a single coin more to be had out of them, they would be arrested. Brutia's instructions were clear. No-Ped suspects were not to be imprisoned till they

had been bled white, their families had sold everything they owned, and there was no gold left to order
new papers. Death offered the only way out, but not
for long. With Tiberius still away fishing in Capri,
Mewlia changed the law so that the houses and valu-
ables of non-pedigrees would automatically pass to
the Emperor after their deaths. It is a bad business and
Brutia was the perfect instrument.

MAIUS XXI

May 21st

A Sleeping Dog's Lies

BRUTIA IS STILL SLEEPING and never comes out
to train with the rest of us.

I am shocked by what I've learned but, looking
at her now, she seems far removed from the terrible
Brutia of old. Fortune had plans for this dog, just like
she had plans for me. It must have happened perhaps
two weeks after I was arrested. Catligula was taking
afternoon drinks with Mewlia in the palace gardens.
Brutia happened to pass them as they were lying
under the shade of a statue of the god Mewpiter. It is
a magnificent statue and looks very fierce. Augustpuss
had it erected after his final victorious campaign in
Purrmania. Catligula looked up as Brutia walked by
and called her over:

'Hey Brutia! I want to ask you a question. Who is
mightier, old Mewpiter here or myself?'

I suppose that Brutia thought he must have been playing. She did not want to offend the god Mewpiter or Catligula with her answer. So she had to think for just a moment before replying that in her opinion, Catligula was greatest. This moment of hesitation was enough for Catligula. He had the Purrmanian bodyguard arrest her for treason. She was overpowered by her own guards and they took her off to prison in a cart.

Brutia has served the Imperial family all her life, first as the protector of the Emperor Tiberius (who had captured her on campaign in Purrmania), then as escort to Mewlia and, most recently, as an escort to Catligula. But Mewlia was the mistress she loved the most. Whether Catligula really meant to arrest her for treason is not clear. He may have meant it as a joke. Or perhaps someone had informed against her that she was fining No-Peds and keeping the money for herself?

Once she was in prison, Fortune spun her another wrong one, for an informer told the authorities that she had 'an overly long body for her breed'. Was there something of the mongrel in her, he wondered. Then the authorities demanded to see her pedigree. And incredible as it may sound, Brutia could not produce one. She herself was a No-Ped. And so she was caught in the jaws of her own trap.

MAIUS XXII

May 22nd

Cell Mates

BRUTIA WOKE EARLIER and barked till the guard arrived. She told them it was disgusting that a noble dog of her nature should be expected to drink from the same water bowl as a flea-ridden animal. That is not true by the way. I am most particular about my fur, even in prison. The guard said he promised to bring her highness Brutia back a silver bowl to drink from, just as soon as he'd spoken to the Father.

At dinner I sat next to a new prisoner called Kitus, who is a No-Ped. He told me that there has been a terrible business with the fish supply. The whole fishing fleet was lost save one ship and now we must send to Fleagypt for dry biscuits instead.

Some are saying that the No-Peds were responsible for this accident and that there should be a crackdown on them for you cannot trust a stray from a feral family. But Kitus says he thinks that the goddess Neptuna is angry with Mewlia for passing such a wicked law, and furious with the Senate for letting her get away with it.

No one at the Senate dares to oppose Mewlia, except old Sarcipuss who says he is so ancient that he has no fear of death.

I must stop writing now because Brutia is stirring.

MEWNONIUS IX

June 9th

An Age of Training

I HAVE HAD NO CHANCE to write for more than two weeks. Our training is exhausting. I have never felt so tired. This is what dogs must feel like. Another reason is Brutia. As I write she is asleep, with her nose between her paws. There is little danger of her waking, so I will take this opportunity to describe our training. Each morning before first light we are woken up by the guards and marched down to the field of exercise – an amphitheatre designed as an exact replica of the Arena. Today they had us running round a training arena wearing heavy iron collars.

After the morning session, guards arrive from the armoury with our weapons. In the first days of training I was particularly uneasy about seeing swords, tridents, and spears at close range. Thankfully all the weapons are made of wood, although they could still do some serious damage. There is always a scramble to pick the best weapons. The law of the jungle applies. Three days running I have been left with a crooked wooden trident but I hope to progress to sword fighting later if I am quicker to leap into the arms pile.

My friend Kitus is convinced that there is a clever illusion going on because, from the seats in the Arena, these wooden weapons appear to be made of the sharpest metal. You can even hear the clang of blade on shield. He wonders how they fake this and how the 'false blood' trick works.

MEWNONIUS X

June 10th

Wooden Swords

I HAVE BEEN THINKING about Kitus' theory about the wooden weapons. At first I dismissed it as ridiculous. But having given it more thought, perhaps there is some truth in it. I have heard it said by many, including Cursus' brother, that gladiatorial contests are carefully stage-managed. He claimed that the fighters are given instructions about how the fight should progress – who should wound whom and at what point, who should appear to be wounded, but recover amazingly and spring up to strike the killer blow, and so on.

We discussed this with Katrin in the kitchen once, as she prepared her fish liquor. I can remember her saying that she didn't care about the fighting or tactics, she was far more interested by the personalities and the dramas that can be witnessed at the Arena.

She said that the best bit was when a brave and noble gladiator called Hercatules (after the god of the gladiators), was pitted against a cowardly, evil, rough villain called Ruffus. This villain almost got the better of Hercatules by means of a dirty trick with his net. It was only when the crowd all called out at once to warn brave Hercatules of his peril that he was saved from a certain spearing. On hearing the hiss of the crowd, at the last minute Hercatules recovered and in an instant he had Ruffus belly up and snared in his own net. It was a classic move according to Saucus, who says he remembers that bout too.

If the outcomes of these battles are predestined, like our lives, then I suppose it makes little difference as long as the crowds are content. They love to see justice done. Whether or not Hercatules is truly a good fighter, he is certainly popular with the females. After the fight they were standing five rows thick around the gates of his villa, waiting for a glimpse of him.

MEWNONIUS XI

June 11th

The Teams are Picked

TODAY OUR TRAINING reached a most exciting stage as we were divided into teams. We were all assembled in columns and the instructors, or Doctors as they are called, came to have a good look at us. These Doctors are retired gladiators and they are respected by everyone here at the school. The first Doctor to inspect us was Puman of Purrsia. He is tall and long limbed, with amber eyes burning out of a proud face. As he walked along the line inspecting us, he flicked the sand with his right paw. Some old ritual or habit perhaps. You could see the claws in his right paw extend, and they were long ones and filed sharp as razors. It is said that he won more than a hundred fights before his retirement but you couldn't tell by the state of his ears and coat which are virtually unmarked. On the basis of this alone, you'd like him for your Doctor.

As Puman stalked down the line, the other Doctors held back. All except one: Dogren of Purrmania. A commanding presence with a huge frame and paws the size of supper plates. His name is known to all in Rome, even those who do not follow the games. He was captured by the Undefeated Legion in the Neuterberger Forest, just across the river Rhine. He'd been caught by means of a trick and dragged back to Rome in chains. They paraded him in triumph and then made him fight for his life in the Arena. He destroyed a succession of opponents. The Emperor Augustpuss was impressed with his bravery. In one bout he thrust his paw into a crocodile's jaw, overpowering the beast. Augustpuss lifted the death sentence and granted Dogren the right to join the gladiatorial school. No one knows his real name, but he is nicknamed Dogren because he seems more dog than cat. He's made over five hundred victorious appearances in the ring and he bears the battle scars all over his body. His ears are all torn and he has leathery marks around the eyes, where deep wounds have closed and healed.

The two Doctors spoke for a moment and then began to pick the teams. As they passed down the line, every prisoner crouched at attention trying to look as fierce as possible. The Doctors looked us over carefully and then nodded to the guards who were carrying pots of red, green, and yellow paint. I am not sure what qualities the Doctors were looking for – perhaps a fierce nature, an undomesticated spirit and so on. Those of my fellows that Doctor Puman picked out were given a daub of red paint on the collar, and those chosen by Dogren received the green mark. It was well known that Catligula supported the greens, and this team looked very 'useful' as my old friend Cursus would say.

The guard with the yellow paint followed down the line after them, taking care of everyone else.

Many of my fellow yellows did appear to be somewhat upset that they had not been selected by either Puman or Dogren. But to the credit of the yellows, they did their best to hide their disappointment. Only a few broke down and wept openly. I told Kitus that it doesn't matter what colour is on our collars. We must play our parts exactly as they have been written. If we work hard and have Fortune's favour, who knows – maybe we'll win the wooden collar of freedom. If not, perhaps we'll find our freedom soon enough, in another way.

MEWNONIUS XII

June 12th

I Become a Net-Cat

MORE TRAINING TODAY and the good news is that we are now free to walk around the training arena unshackled although we are still locked into our cells at night. Brutia is training separately. Who knows what she is doing!

This morning I assembled with the other yellows in our training area. We were told that we yellows are to be trained as Net-Cats or 'Fraidipusses' as they are sometimes called by the crowds. Apparently it is a specialist fighting tradition. We have no armour to weigh us down and our only weapons are the net and the three-pronged trident. Some of us already have some knowledge of the games and, according to them, our principal tactic is to become expert judges of what is known as the 'danger area'. This is the area where you are within striking range of your opponent. Our tactic must be to flee from this area as swiftly as possible and not stop running till our opponent is worn out.

We have no net and trident instructor yet due to a shortage of qualified teachers willing to take us on. But in the meantime, we have been told to practise running away.

MEWNONIUS XIII

June 13th

Pity the Fraidipuss!

EVERYONE SAYS THAT it is not a good thing to be a Fraidipuss. It would be nobler to be one of Dogren's team with their curved scimitars, round shields and heavy helmets. Or perhaps to be one of the Purmillo – who are armed with a gladius and a square shield. They are at an advantage because the public immediately recognises their fighting style from the legions.

I had hoped that we might be liked by some section of the crowd, fish eaters perhaps, because of our tridents. But Kitus tells me that we Fraidipusses are at a disadvantage. The crowd likes their gladiators to stand and fight, no matter how great the danger. The crowd is, for the most part, uneducated, so this ignorance of tactics of the games does not surprise me. But I am ashamed to admit that there are even some of our own yellow number who seem to agree with that view and are disgusted at themselves. A fighting style based on running away until your opponent is too exhausted to chase you – and then taunting them from a safe distance with your spear, suits me perfectly. We don't wear defensive armour and so have the advantage against our heavily armed opponents when it comes to speed of flight. Besides, we cannot all be Furasians, or Purmillo. As one of the guards says, we are needed in order to show some variety because 'styles make fights' as he put it. I'm unsure about the exact meaning of this. I shall have to ask Cursus, if I ever see him again.

At any rate, until we get an instructor, I shall keep practising running away whenever there is the slightest hint of danger (which is often in this place).

The one good thing about being a yellow is our special diet. Whilst the reds and greens are on raw fish and lean meat, the diet of the yellows is fried chicken and as many bowls of cream as we can eat.

MEWNONIUS XIV

June 14th

TODAY WE YELLOWS were provided with nets but we still don't have an instructor.

There were four accidents today, including a couple of painful entanglements.

But when we saw the other teams training, we began to think that we're getting a better deal of it. Dogren's team has been issued with weapons and armour that are three times as heavy as the real ones. They are made of iron and have been made heavier still using lead and concrete. I could not understand why but one of my fellows, a tom called Leapus, explained that this was to build up their strength, so that when they pick up their real weapons, they will find it easy to fight. Tomorrow we plan to weigh ourselves down with concrete collars in order to make us faster at running away.

As for Brutia, she is still not training with us. Have they picked her out for some special event perhaps? She ignores my attempts to get her talking.

MEWNONIUS XV

June 15th

MY POOR NECK! I think that the concrete collar I wore yesterday has cut into it and done me lasting damage. Today I shall swap it for a copper one, which Kitus says is therapeutic, although I am not so sure.

I am beginning to fear that I am not learning my new skills fast enough. I am not bad at running away, but I haven't got the hang of my net or my trident. In fact the net is useless. I keep netting myself instead of my opponent. 'It's all in the action of the paw,' I am told by everyone who watches me throw the net. But quite what this paw action may be, none can explain.

Whilst wondering about this with Kitus, who is almost as useless with the net as I am, I remembered the notices in the entrance hall to the canteen about the personal training. We went back to read them and Kitus was very struck by the notice of Bogan the Trayjan. Then I saw that the last notice had been taken down. I could clearly see where it had been, just below

Bogan's notice. I remembered that the missing notice had said something about 'Unharmed Combat' and the Doctor's name was Tefnut. I have decided to make enquiries.

MEWNONIUS XVI

June 16th

Training with the Trayjan

KITUS WAS GOING TO ENROL on Dogren's training course about 'Making an End of It'. I told him that dying lessons sound like waste of money, but he said that it is bound to be useful at some time or other. I have pointed him towards 'Win the Crowd and Win Your Freedom'.

As for myself, I have decided to find Tefnut and get some lessons, although this may be more difficult than I thought.

According to Kitus, Tefnut has been banned from teaching because some of her methods are said to be 'unfeline'. She teaches tricks that are an offence to the good name of the honest gladiator. On the orders of the Father, she is no longer allowed to advertise her lessons. But her notices still pop up in unexpected places. If Kitus means to discourage me with this, then he has had the opposite effect. I am now even more determined to find Tefnut and learn whatever I can from her.

MEWNONIUS XVII

June 17th

A Cold Snap

BRUTIA IS GETTING BETTER. She snapped at me quite viciously last night after I accidentally disturbed her blanket whilst climbing down from my bunk. It was a brush of the tail and no more, but her attack was so fierce that I had to climb up to the window-sill to get out of biting distance. She scoffed at me, saying

'Observe the mighty Spartapuss! Come down here gladiator and we shall do battle.'

I made no answer to this but you can imagine that I didn't want to fight her. My new running away skills wouldn't be any use in a tiny cell.

'Come down hero. You felt like a big cat when you beat Liccus in combat. But now you're frightened. I can smell it,' she growled.

I must be honest now and say that what she could smell was probably not my fear. It is hot for those of us who are thicker of fur, and the bathing facilities aren't as good as the ones back at the spa.

I decided to stay put until she calmed down. As for courage, I have little, so I'll have to get by with what the gods have given me. I don't want to use it up all at once!

MEWNONIUS XVIII

June 18th

A Shortage of Doctors

THE FESTIVAL OF PURRCURY draws nearer. And we yellows have no doctor to instruct us. I have asked all over the school for news of Tefnut, but no one has a clue about her comings and goings. However I have learned from Kitus that the armourer, Nailus, may know how to contact her. He mends weapons for all the doctors, apparently.

MEWNONIUS XIX

June 19th

In the Armoury

TODAY BRUTIA was protesting to the guards that it is wrong for a dog of her noble nature to be kept in the same cell as a filthy Kiton slave like myself. I don't think they'll listen to her, but I dearly hope that her wish is granted. My tail is still smarting after another unprovoked attack this morning.

My search for Tefnut continues. I went to the armoury to see if there was any word of her. I found the armourer, Nailus, hard at work sharpening an axe, which belongs to none other than Bogan the Trayjan. He explained he 'does' all the weapons for the Doctors personally. They are all very particular about how the sharpening is done. Some have given their weapons names and they even talk to them before they go to sleep, or whisper secret prayers to them before they do battle.

Nailus thinks that all weapons are possessed with spirits. 'Axes have the strongest spirit for battle,' he says. Bogan's axe is called Arnia, after his first love. Bogan's instructions are very precise. Arnia has a double-sided blade – most unusual for an axe – as they are blunt implements of battle, made for the crushing of bones and the pounding of brains. So what was the point of a double-edge on an axe blade? Only a Trayjan would think of that. Mind you, Nailus wasn't going to argue with Bogan. If he wanted to call it Axe-ligula and instructed Nailus to sharpen its wooden hilt, then Nailus wouldn't question his orders.

On seeing the yellow on my collar, he shook his head and began to give me advice on how to pick out a good trident. The shafts are all of slightly differing lengths and it is best to choose one of medium length for the best balance between manoeuvrability and reach. But then again, a long one helps you to stay out of harm's way. The shafts themselves are made of many particular types of wood – some of ash, some of oak and some of willow. Willow gives the best balance of strength and flexibility but be careful not to choose one of the Maulish willow, for they are poor trees and no mistaking it. I did not think it possible that the shaft of a trident would be the subject of a conversation, which could last more than half an hour. Moreover, he made the topic of the prongs of a trident last an extra fifteen minutes. By the time he was done, the blade of Bogan's axe was as sharp as a shark's tooth.

It is very hot in the armoury and I was panting like a hound by the time I left. My yellow dye had started to run. I asked if Tefnut ever brought her weapons in. All of a sudden, Nailus went quiet and shook his head.

Didn't she use the armoury at the School? I asked. Perhaps she had her own sharpener? Nailus looked surprised for a moment before replying:

'Tefnut doesn't fight with weapons like these. She has no need of them.'

'But you must see her around the School some times?' I asked, a little desperately.

Nailus said he was sorry, but he knew nothing of the whereabouts of Tefnut.

It was clear that I could get no more out of him, so I left him to his sharpening.

I was no nearer to finding my instructor.

MEWNONIUS XX

June 20th

Drilled to Kill

TODAY AT TRAINING, Kitus went on and on about Dogren's team and the fabulous education that they are receiving. Apparently they are being taught in the classical fighting style and they spend all day doing exercises known as 'kill drills'. With these they practise their moves one after the other. High thrust – block, low thrust – block, swipe, claw, pound, dirt in the face, high thrust – block and so on.

I told him that I was pleased to hear that they are all doing so well at it, at least one group of fighters would be well trained enough to hold up the good name of our school. My yellow team mates had been taking full advantage of the cream and fried chicken on offer, and were looking tamer every day. I decided to take my leave of Kitus and continue my search for Tefnut.

So far, she has been impossible to find. But I learned much at my previous academy, Spatopia. Certain members of the household knew all of Clawdius' secrets. If anyone has any information about the whereabouts of Tefnut, it must surely be the cleaners. They must walk every step of the ludus daily and clean everywhere (apart from that storage area by the forge, which looks extremely grubby – I must remember to remind them of it). So I decided to seek out their advice.

By the laundry, I found them, on a break. They were discussing the topic of crime and punishment. The general view was that law and order is a terrible problem in Rome and that things have been getting worse and worse since the old days of the Repurrblic. The only answer was to parade criminals through the streets, then tie them in a sack and throw them into the river. This would be a good way of getting rid of bad rubbish. But for really bad crimes, the prisoners should be hung upside down from a pole for weeks and thrown to the wild beasts at the games. Apparently the small beasts, such as rats, voles and parrots, are the cruellest executioners because they take their time.

All the cleaners thought that this was a splendid solution, except for one, called Isis, who kept quiet. When asked to give her view, she suggested that executions should not be staged at the games because it was wrong to turn justice into entertainment for the crowds. This brought waves of laughter from the rest of the cleaners. It is a rather unusual point of view, and one that reminded me of the sort of thing that Russell often used to come out with back at the spa.

When a pause in the conversation arrived, I approached and introduced myself.

It was clear by their reaction that some of them were not happy to be seen talking to a gladiator. We are the very lowest kind of slaves – lower than strays even. When I mentioned Tefnut, the group fell silent. No one could aid me in my quest, save for a cleaner called Isis.

Her green eyes held me for a moment in a deep gaze that made me feel a little uncomfortable. She said that she might be able to give me some information regarding Tefnut. However, the tradition where she came from said that there should be a payment of one gold coin for any information given. I asked where she came from – the rest of them seemed to find it very funny indeed and laughed. 'Why, Fleagypt of course,' said a tabby, 'can't you tell by the collar?'

At the mention of Fleagypt, Isis gave the tabby a hard stare.

When I explained that I had no money to offer, only my gratitude, they laughed even more. Isis said that she understood my problem. Then she offered me a job in an ancient and noble profession (that some found enjoyable). The rate of pay would be one gold coin a month. I could start my new job this very night. I thanked her most sincerely and I soon agreed.

Then I asked her if I could perhaps have some money in advance, in order to pay for the information I needed about Tefnut. She told me that I would qualify for a loan if I could make a decent job of it throughout this week. But she warned me that it was hard work that takes effort to do properly. Many who start give up before mastering it.

'Careful sister, this ginger looks like a born quitter, I can see it in his markings,' said one of the cleaners.

I ignored this and agreed to meet Isis in the training arena after dinner. My duties will begin tonight.

MEWNONIUS XXI

June 21st

An Ancient Craft

IF I HAD THE ENERGY, I would raise a paw to salute the skill and devotion of the Ancient Craft of the Ring Rakers. For this is the profession that I have joined.

Isis says that we gladiators step into the Arena (or the 'ring' as she calls it) with thoughts in our head: thoughts of glory, of death, of honour and so on. But in our rush towards immortality, we never spare a thought for the efforts of those who have worked so hard on our account, preparing a beautiful fighting surface under our paws.

The sand of the Arena floor gets filthy with the blood, sweat and sometimes worse. So it must be raked over thoroughly. It's the only way to get a good fighting surface for the games. This is done with wooden rakes, and the crossed rakes are the symbol of the Ancient Craft of the Ring Rakers. And now I, Spartapuss, have joined them.

It seems to be a very worthy profession. It is quite easy for beginners to take up because no equipment is needed except a rake and the will to keep on going until the job is done.

MEWNONIUS XXII

June 22nd

Raking Delays

UNFORTUNATELY THERE IS a shortage of rakes. According to Isis, the supply ship that brings them from Fleagypt was sunk in a heavy storm and none of the cleaners will lend me one of theirs. Isis says that I'll have to start my ring-raking training using my trident instead. It is not ideal, but I suppose it will have to do.

Despite this snag, I am in good spirits. The only problem is Brutia. She has got into the habit of speaking to me every night, last thing before I go to sleep. The topic is always the same – how I will meet my death in the Arena in just a few days' time. The details vary from night to night. Last night she had me torn limb-from-limb by a pack of starving wolves with stinking breath and yellow fangs that ripped my flesh. The night before I was crushed beneath the wheels of her battle chariot, my skull giving way like an eggshell under the weight of her spiked left wheel. Unfortunately she has a very detailed imagination, and paints such pictures, that it takes a great effort on my part not to carry them into my dreams. So I shall try to block them out with pleasant visions of my own. Tonight I shall imagine myself eating a delicious fish supper.

MEWNONIUS XXIII

June 23rd

The Group of Death

WE YELLOWS STILL don't have an instructor. Morale is low. Some of the others just stuff their faces and sleep through running away practice. Kitus told me yesterday that the others have started calling our team 'the group of death'. His brother Katus is in the red team. He was picked by Puman on account of his superior teeth and coat condition (much to the disappointment of poor Kitus). He says that even if a willing Doctor could be found to train us, it would probably be too late for us to get good enough to survive the combat. The reds and the greens are way ahead of us now and can fight confidently with sword, shield, and claw to claw. Dogren's green team in particular is making good progress and members continue with their 'kill drills'. Meanwhile, the Purmillo have been practising their 'death charges'. Katus says it looked hard at first but you get used to it. The red mist of battle gets into your eyes and you just go wild when the hissing starts.

Brutia has a good imagination for bad things. She says she is saving the best details of my death for tonight's bedtime story. I'll continue to ignore her. The imagination is a great sculptor so it's a good job that my mind is too thick to chip with a chisel! My final thought before sleep tonight will be that delicious fish supper, which I didn't have time to finish last night. But now I must slip out for some more raking practice, as I don't want to keep Isis waiting. My duties continue every evening. Isis crouches patiently, watching my every movement intently, as if something exciting is just about to happen. It is as if she has never seen anyone rake sand before. It is filthy work toiling with four paws in the sand and the grit gets everywhere – right under my pads.

MEWNONIUS XXV

June 25th

Yellows Alert

YOU DON'T HAVE TO LOOK for pawtents to see that Fortune has spun us yellows a wrong one. Apparently some of Katus' group are proving so promising with their swords that they may soon progress to instructions from Bogan in the art of beating the opponent's brains out with the battle-axe.

The only instruction that I've managed to find is in raking of sand. Tonight I got the job done in good time in order to please Isis. I may be a Fraidipuss and a poor gladiator but surely I can be a ring raker, for no skills are required! There are still no rakes available so I'm using my trident. It's not as good as a proper rake because it cuts furrows in the sand and throws it all over the place. But I really flew at the task this time, turning over the sand in broad strips. It is hot work and halfway through, I confess that I thought I was not going to make it. But I finished the job in about three hours. Isis had disappeared by the time I'd finished, but I hope she'll be pleased with it.

MEWNONIUS XXVI

June 26th

I Try to Please Isis

IN THE NAME OF THE GODDESS, Isis takes some pleasing. She's the pickiest cleaner I've ever met. This morning she told me that my approach displeased her greatly and that I had better pay attention carefully or I would never make a proper raker. She said I was upsetting the Arena with my movements and that it is the way of the ring raker to please the sand with your steps, not trample it all over the place and insult it. This is most unfair. She only watched me for few minutes before leaving. What possible difference can it make how you tread on the sand if you are about to rake it over?

I was close to giving in, but I agreed to return tonight. I have no alternative if I want to earn that gold coin.

Brutia says she has a really good bedtime story for me tonight but I am becoming quite good at ignoring her. Tonight I shall focus on a fresh fish dinner. We have not had fresh fish since we arrived. It is the tradition that the groups must all sit on their separate tables and that the yellows must serve the other teams before getting their own food. It fell to poor Kitus to serve his brother Katus who sits on Puman's table. The tradition is that the servers must remain silent or receive a beating. Yet the looks they exchanged said everything. From Kitus the yellow, there was sorrow and a tiny flick of envy – from Katus the red there was embarrassment to have a brother as a yellow, and guilt that there was nothing he could do to help.

MEWNONIUS XXVII

June 27th

There's No Pleasing Some Cleaners

YET ANOTHER CRUEL SPIN from Fortune's wheel! Isis is proving to be impossible to please. Never have I known a cleaner so particular in her attention to details. Tonight I raked the whole ring in under two and a half hours, and yet her only comment was a criticism about the way that I hold my rake, which isn't even a proper rake anyway, it's a trident (as I reminded her). What possible difference does it make how I hold the 'rake', as long as I get the job done?

MEWNONIUS XXVIII

June 28th

Patterns in the Sand

ISIS WAS A BIT BETTER PLEASED with my work today. I asked her how I should begin my practice, and she replied that I should 'start it as I thought best.' She watched in silence as I tried to copy the way she did it yesterday. I was raking in an even sweeping motion, keeping my balance, and taking great care not to tread on any of the sand that had been raked over already. Treading on the bits you've done spoils the pattern. Isis says that I've proved that I can 'please the sand with my steps', which I suppose must be a good thing. But I'm starting to think I shall never understand her or any of the cleaners here for that matter. Their ways are mysterious. I thought that I'd finished with raking but tomorrow the first of what Isis calls 'the ancient patterns' will be revealed to me. There are many to learn and I hope she doesn't expect me to learn all of them at once.

MEWNONIUS XXIX

June 29th

TODAY I WENT RING RAKING during the day as well as during the night. We Fraidipusses are unsupervised and, although it is tempting to lounge upon the cushion all day, there is much to learn. Kitus asked where I was going, and I wondered if I should tell him what I've been doing, only it is a little embarrassing especially as I still don't have a rake and I have to use my wooden trident. So I told him that I have found a nice spot for a sleep down by the armoury. I feel for him, but what he fears most, might not happen. The names of the fighters for the games are to be drawn by lots. If he is drawn against his brother then it will be Fortune's will.

I found Isis in her usual place, sitting upright and still. She watches the world go by as if she's asleep with her eyes wide open. Perhaps she's concentrating very hard on some detail of the sand that I cannot see. Cleaners have eyes that spot all manner of marks that remain hidden to the rest of us.

She wasn't surprised to see me arrive for a lesson at midday. She just told me to put down my trident and pay attention. Then she padded across the sand, doing a funny little dance. First she leapt forwards and then she jumped back a couple of steps in a start-stop, start-stop manner. She looked quite ridiculous and I almost burst out laughing.

As she moved across the ring, her tail flicked left and right, swishing strange sweeping patterns in the sand behind her. It was one of the strangest things I've ever seen. At one point she almost rolled to the floor as if she was about to stumble, like a ferret sometimes does when chasing a hare. I was about to offer her a paw up when something strange happened. She twisted her whole body, somersaulted and appeared again, having righted herself perfectly with the rake in her other paw. Clouds of sand shot across the Arena and for a moment I lost sight of her in all the dust.

When it cleared, I saw that she'd left a snaking pattern in the sand. She explained that ring raking is a practice dating back many years and there are a variety of patterns to be made in the sand, all of them symbolic. This one was called 'The Shifting Dunes'. I am to start learning it tomorrow.

I fear that she has spent too many years raking in the hot sand and it has burned the wits out of her brain. For after telling me this, she drew close and whispered that all these patterns are secret, and I am never to speak of them to those outside our order.

I replied that I didn't know anyone else in our order, apart from her, but I could be relied upon not to tell another soul.

It all seems rather pointless (although I did not say this, of course). Neither we gladiators nor the public give a moment's thought to the marks on the sand of the Arena floor. All of her efforts are wasted! Her pretty patterns are trampled into the dust as soon as the fighting starts.

MEWNONIUS XXX

June 30th

The Shifting Dunes

TODAY ISIS BEGAN to teach me my first pattern. 'The Shifting Dunes' is hard to perform because the positions of the body are quite unnatural. Also I imagine that my trident is heavier than the true rake that a master raker of the order would use. At first I could think of nothing but falling on my face. So I did. Three times. Then Isis stopped me for a word of advice. She reminded me to please the sand with my steps. I told her that I could not seem to find my steps but, in the meantime, I would have to continue to please the sand with my face. With a serious glare she told me that I was trying too hard. I had to think of something else, in order to take my mind off the complexity of the movements. Now, one thing that I am very good at is not thinking about things. This is a gift I have had all my life and apparently it is quite common amongst us Kitons. I have had a lot of practice recently because of Brutia's horrible bedtime stories.

For some reason, I pictured a fishing boat, its sails billowing in the wind. I held this in my mind's eye as I danced through the pattern. A little leap forward, dodge left and right, then back and forth in a start-stop manner, sweep with the tail, trident into the right paw and weight onto the left side, stumble as if to fall and then rotate your body. I found myself rolling out, still in rhythm, with the trident now in my left paw. When the dust cloud cleared, a strange snaking pattern was left in the sand behind me. I had recovered from the fall and executed my first 'Shifting Dunes'. Isis called it a perfect manoeuvre but she worried me a little when she asked, 'Were you thinking of the storm as you stepped?'

Without waiting for my answer, she laughed and said, 'Good! Tomorrow there will be fire.'

CATILIS I

July 1st

The Bleached Bones

LAST NIGHT I dreamed of deserts, then of a fish dinner, then of being sucked to death by the gums of a giant fish. I think it was a cod. Perhaps I will choose another image instead of fish to shut out Brutia's bedtime story tonight.

Today Isis walked me through the steps of 'The Shifting Dunes' a couple of times, saying that method of practice should help me master the patterns without thinking. I told her that I was an expert at not thinking, according to Master Clawdius. After seeing me walk through 'The Shifting Dunes' a couple of times she was happy with it, and we moved on to my second pattern, called 'The Bleached Bones'.

This pattern is a prayer to the sun god. It was exhausting to hear Isis describe it. The young sun sits flaming in the sky. He burns away at the bodies of the fallen until not a scrap of flesh remains and the desert swallows their bones. He grows old but still he continues to burn and will not leave the heavens, for he would burn everything if he could. So the goddess brings him down with a spear and her followers haul him down under the world. And his sister Moon rules in his place for the night. Or was it his mother who was the moon? At any rate, I felt sorry for the sun and I was going to ask Isis how he gets back in the sky, but there was no time.

She began the dance with a step back, dummying as if to move left but then going right, as she beat the ground in rhythm. Then she beckoned me to follow her into the ring. As I sat before her, I started to feel queasy, perhaps because of last night's field-mouse supper, which didn't agree with me. As she moved, I thought I could hear cymbals and drums beating far away. Doom-shakka-lak, doom-shakka-lakka. I lost my concentration for a moment. The heat was unbearable. The next thing I remember was being buried up to my neck in sand. How it happened, I cannot tell. I apologised and Isis laughed. She has promised to teach me how to do this pattern properly tomorrow. In the confusion, I forgot to ask her about the gold coin I need to buy the information about Tefnut.

The festival of Purrcury is drawing near.

CATILIS II

July 2nd

Magic or Sand Rats?

I'M NOT SUPERSTITIOUS by nature but I can't think of any way to explain what happened at ring raking practice today.

We began as usual, only this time Isis walked out into the centre of the training arena and stood in front of me leaning on her rake, and fixing me with that stare of hers. I worked steadily through the steps that she'd taught me. As my trident beat the sand, the galley of my thoughts let slip its moorings, and I imagined that I could hear distant music. I was so drawn into the pattern that I stopped only when I found that Isis had vanished into the sand in front of me. Only the end of her rake was still to be seen. In a panic, I called out to her, digging like a dog with my back paws into the place where she had disappeared. I am not sure, but I imagine that burying your instructor in the arena probably isn't one of the traditions in the Ancient Order of Ring Rakers. I searched frantically but Isis was nowhere to be found.

Then the strangest thing happened. She appeared to rise from out of the centre of the ring, the sand flying away from her as if blown by a whirlwind. I apologised for burying her. I thought that she'd be furious but instead she was pleased and told me I'd done well.

'We'll make a raker of you yet!' she said. But she would teach me no more today, saying that I looked too tired to start to learn 'The Salt Tears' today. So that will have to wait until tomorrow. Isis says that I'm doing well for a beginner, having almost mastered two of the first three patterns.

As I write, I wonder whether the remarkable event of Isis' burial and reappearance could be a pawtent like the ones you hear about in stories. I can think of no other explanation, apart from sand rats like the ones that we used to get in the spa. They dig deep tunnels and maybe Isis was standing on the sand above one of their burrows, which must have collapsed. If it really was a pawtent then I have no idea what it can mean.

CATILISIII

July 3rd

The Salt Tears

ON THE WAY to my practice today, my path was blocked by an excited crowd that had assembled in the exercise yard. I caught sight of Kitus, who explained that the fighting list had been put up, and that some trouble had broken out. A dreadful hissing and growling was going up. Apparently, just moments before I arrived, there had been a fight to see who should read the list first. This was broken up by the guards when it looked as if some serious damage was about to be done. They reminded us that we were the property of the school and should not damage each other before the games.

Kitus said that he couldn't get near the list to look at it. Some Furasians had started a scuffle with the yellows. They said that we fat Fraidipusses had better keep out of their sight if we wanted to live to see the festival of Purrcury. One of them said that he would give his life for the honour of the green team, before letting us yellows see the list before them. So here we are, all prisoners and slaves together, half of us guaranteed to die within the week. And some of us are fighting about colours and who gets to read a list first!

I am not fierce by nature and have never won a fight, apart from the one against Liccus on the day of my capture, but I must confess that I was so angry at this stupidity that I began to bristle. Poor Kitus was terrified that he would be made to fight against his brother Katus.

I left him waiting to read the list for I had an appointment with Isis. She was not pleased with my patterns. I was finding it hard to concentrate and could think of nothing but how badly poor Kitus had been treated. I told her what had happened

'They are afraid,' she said. 'Fear makes them dangerous.'

But she warned me not to get angry, for it is 'an unreliable master.'

I had no clue what she meant by this but it was

time to move onto my third pattern: 'The Salt Tears'. This time Isis' movements were slow and mournful. She circled with her body low to the ground as she flicked the dry sand with her tail. It looked pitiful. My thoughts ran to the Arena. I remembered that I am condemned to fight. Then I recalled that it was also my birthday and that I am so far away from my friends. I felt tears rise up and as I went to rub my eyes, they started to burn so intensely that I was completely blinded. It was only after some minutes rubbing that my vision gradually returned.

'How do you do that?' I asked.

'This pattern collects your fears in the salt of your tears. When you cry they are released. Sometimes the salt is very concentrated: if it's too much to bear, you are blinded,' she said.

CATILIS IV

July 4th

Lots Are Drawn

GOOD NEWS. Kitus must fight one of Dogren's team, and not his brother Katus who is one of Puman's reds. I am also matched against a Furasian called Hissero, whom I know nothing about, but it looks like a good draw. Kitus says he's a big bag of fur who was arrested for poaching carp from the municipal lake in order to make it into pies. We yellows are all praying that we will be drawn against large, lumbering opponents so that our principal battle tactic – running away, will work. One surprise though, Brutia's name is not on the list.

There are just seven days till the Games of Purrcury, so I will speak to Isis about the loan of a gold coin tomorrow.

CATILIS V

July 5th

Three Bad Spins from Fortune's Wheel

TODAY WENT ILL on three counts. Firstly yesterday's draw for the gladiatorial games was declared void. This means that there will be a redraw. A new list will be announced tomorrow following a visit from the Imperial draw-master. The second count involved Brutia. Yesterday we noticed that she was not named on the combat list. Apparently she was most disappointed to find her name had been omitted from it due to a clerical error. So she went for clerk of the lists and bit through his tail, right down to the bone! Instead of punishing her, the Father has put her name on the list, and now she will fight a demonstration match against a gladiator chosen specially by the Patron of the Games – none other than Catligula himself. Thirdly, when I turned up for ring raking practice today there was no sign of Isis. Her usual spot, in the shadow of the concrete steps, was empty. I was at a loss about what to do for a while, but then I decided to start stepping through some patterns on my own, in the hope that she'd arrive later. It was unlike her to be late, she's one of the most regular cats I've ever known.

I'd been hard at practice for about an hour when Isis finally arrived. After making the three successful patterns as instructed, I asked her about the money. She can be hard to read sometimes. She was surprised that I was still interested in finding Tefnut to get training. But, true to her promise, she unhooked a coin from her collar straight away. It was gold but not one of ours, probably Fleagyptian. Although she was happy to lend me the money, she's proving to be a rather unreliable source of information. With gold coin in paw, I asked her solemnly if I could purchase information on the whereabouts of the infamous Doctor Tefnut, for the sum of one gold coin. She said that she could tell me two things for certain:

That Tefnut was near, but Tefnut was impossible to contact save by means of a sand message.

This convinced me that all those years raking in a hot Arena have baked her brains. She is obsessed with sand! But she gave me a watchword, which she claims will summon Tefnut. Apparently I am to write the word in large letters in the sand of the ring and wait there till Tefnut arrives. But sand messages can only work when the moon is full. Surely this is final proof that Isis has been raking too long! Kitus says that she may be after my money but I don't have any, save for the gold coin, which I earned from her by ring raking. At any rate, there is no full moon for some three nights hence, so my message must wait until then.

CATILIS VI

July 6th

Brother Against Brother

POOR KITUS! His worst fears have come to be. It is as if he wished them true by trying to wish them away. He is now matched against his brother Katus in the games.

This morning we were called to assemble in the main yard, in full fighting order. About half of the Fraidipusses, including Kitus and I, were called aside and told to put down our tridents. Then they dressed us up as Purmillos, complete with fish shaped helmets and short swords. This caused uproar amongst the other teams but the guards soon shut them up with the threat of the red-hot iron. The guards shackled us all together to prevent any more trouble.

Earlier that morning, a rumour had gone about that visitors were arriving to inspect us. So it was no surprise that they were going to the effort of getting us all kitted out neatly. But we can only guess at the reasons behind the switching of yellows for greens and reds. Yesterday's draw had been declared a void, because of a technicality. The proper sacrifices and prayers had not been given to Hercatules. However, some were saying that the true reason for this was that when Mewlia saw the list, she suspected the Father of rigging the draw in order to give the best gladiators a safe passage. The Father does not want to lose two good fighters in every bout – so he was seeking to match a Fraidipuss against a Furasian or a Purmillo wherever possible. That way the fights would be quick and bloody, ending without expensive injuries or the loss of his best fighters. Who would be a Fraidipuss! But it seemed that someone here learned of this and sold the news to Mewlia. Catligula went into a fury, tearing an ear off the messenger. They have demanded an audience with the Father and an inspection in order to pick out the fighters themselves.

But the Father has eyes and ears in the palace, and someone must have tipped him off. That is why Kitus and I were now dressed up as Purmillos, even though neither of us is any good with a sword!

A green chariot pulled up with Mewlia and Catligula in it. This was the first time I had set eyes on Catligula since my imprisonment and there was a glint in his eye that said he had grown wilder still. For a moment I feared that he would recognise me but my face was hidden under the visor of my helmet.

The Father arrived first, carried in a sedan chair by a couple of gladiators in full armour. Dogren and Puman greeted him respectfully. They approached with their tails down and neither would look him fully in the eyes. Dogren showed a special respect. I learned later that the Father had personally bought him his freedom when he won his two hundredth fight. Dogren had then joined the school as a Doctor, swearing an oath to defend the Father with his life.

Despite this protection, and the knowledge that he commanded enough trained gladiators to assemble a private army, the Father looked uneasy in Mewlia's presence. Catligula glared at him, paying no attention to us slaves. From my position in the front row I could hear exactly what was said.

'Fine warriors your highnesses. And all of them trained under the guidance of Rome's best Doctors. Rarely has such a fine group of fighting felines been assembled for selection. Each of them a peach, each picked by my own paw.'

'Father Felinius, save your patter for the fools who usually come in here. Peus knows that these 'peaches' are criminals and strays under sentence of death.'

'Your Highness, you have been misled. I would not argue with your nobility but these are the greatest fighting ...'

'You boast like a common fish seller, Felinius, but your catch is rotten. It stinks.' hissed Catligula.

His look stopped Felinius in his tracks. The Father knew that any quarrel with the Imperial family would prove a mismatch.

'Do not dispute with us Father,' said Mewlia. 'We know that some of these convicts have not received their basic training. Are you still short of trident teach-ers?"

The Father remained silent. He was stunned at the quality of their information. Their spies were every-where.

Mewlia passed the Father a new list. Catligula warned him not to complain, lest he himself should fight the Father in the first bout!

At last, Felinious looked up and spoke.

'I see you want battle chariots in the style of the Kitons. I'm sure that can be arranged.'

'There was far too much arranging in the last draw,' said Mewlia.

The Father beckoned to Dogren. The huge gladia-tor padded to his side.

'Do we have any Kitons who have mastery of the battle chariot?' he asked.

'Kitons, make yourselves known now,' called Dogren.

The Father apologised again, saying that he was rather low on Kitons, but adding that they can still be secured by Kiton slavers, although they are overpriced for what they are. Catligula was not in the mood for excuses.

'For Peus' sake! Are any of you Kitons or can you drive a chariot? Speak, or I shall have every one of you executed from... tail to tail,' hissed Catligula.

'Lord, we have a Spartapuss listed...' began Dogren.

'I don't want a Spartan! I want a Kiton!' raged

Catligula.

'Spartapuss is a Kiton, or a half-Kiton at least,' explained Felinious. I was amazed that he remembered me, but the Father knew everything about every gladiator in his stable.

'Spartapuss – make yourself known!' yelled Dogren.

My heart froze in my chest. It was happening again.

'Where is Spartapuss?'

'Step forward Spartapuss!'

'Spar-ta-puss!' 'Spar-ta-puss!' came the shouts.

This time I didn't bother to ask Fortune what I'd done to offend her.

'I am Spartapuss,' I said. 'And I am a Kiton. But I'm afraid I have no experience in the chariot.'

'Sir, he is the fastest learner amongst us and I'm sure he should pick up chariot racing very quickly,' added Kitus on my behalf.

Catligula put down a dormouse kebab that he had been sucking and began to study me closely. I thanked Mewpiter that the helmet covered my face from his glare.

'I suppose he'll do,' he hissed.

'An excellent choice, Highness. But now for an opponent! Who shall we match this six-clawed Kiton against?'

'We have plenty of net and trident fighters available,' said the clerk checking his list.

'How about this Kiton, in his armoured chariot, against ten fighters with net and trident?'

Mewlia rolled her eyes.

'Really Felonious, you'd better come up with something better than that. Those flea-ridden Fraidipusses couldn't fight their way out of a ball of wool if you armed them with double-edged scissors.'

Then Catligula moved close to Mewlia and whispered in her ear. They both started to laugh, and I was surprised that Mewlia's laughter was almost kittenish.

'The opponent we have in mind is a prisoner here,' said Catligula. The Father nodded.

'We shall send word,' said Mewlia.

And with that we were all dismissed.

I can only guess the fate they have planned for me when I enter through the Gate of Death. I'm beginning to expect the worst at every spin of Fortune's wheel.

As we changed back into our usual clothes, I took Kitus aside for a word in private. He said that he was resolved to escape rather than fight his own brother to the death in the Arena. I offered to help if I could.

He asked my opinion on his first escape plan. He would build a machine to fling him over the Western Wall to freedom. This machine, called a ballista, is used in the military, apparently with some success. Only their main purpose is to fling concrete shot, bags of fleas or the heads of the fallen back upon the enemy. I said I thought it was an interesting idea but the construction of such a machine would be sure to attract the attention of the guards. Kitus says he will give this some more thought.

CATILIS VII

July 7th

The Prisoner's Death

HAVING TO LISTEN to Brutia describing my death every night has been bad enough. But on the way back to the cells after raking practice, she sprang directly for my throat without warning. Before her jaws could get a good grip, Fortune spun me a good one. A couple of guards were passing. They saw what was happening and dragged her off me, telling us to save our energy for the Arena. The best news of all is that she's been moved to another cell.

Now at least I can sleep easier at night, although I have become very good at visualising delicious foods prior to sleeping. I started doing this to avoid Brutia's dreadful descriptions. She described 'the prisoners' death the night before last, which is where you are hung upside down and... Well, I will not go into details. She talked about this for hours, but I remember none of it, for my mind was on fish sauce as I pictured Katrin cooking a pie back at the spa.

Now I must retire. I begin chariot training at dawn.

Kitus has abandoned the plan involving the ballista, for it turns out that he is has a terrible fear of heights. So he has decided to dig a tunnel under the Western Wall instead.

CATILIS VIII

July 8th

Chariots Charge

I SLEPT WELL last night and woke up early for chariot training feeling refreshed.

Two guards took me to the new chariot area, which is on the other side of the school. Everyone knows that chariots usually race at the circus but the Father has created a special practice track for us here at the ludus.

As I padded across the grounds, I noticed many gates painted red or green. These were special training areas for the Furasians and Purmillo. No Fraidipusses has ever set paw in these areas before.

Through a half open gate, I glimpsed a group of Furasians. They were charging at a revolving wooden post. Close by, a second group was drilling their sword strokes. They fought well considering that they were weighed down by heavy armour. Catligula will not be disappointed by his Games, by the look of this.

At last we arrived at a fenced enclosure perhaps three or four times larger than the exercise yard in Spatopia. We were met by a tall fellow, a Kiton like myself by the look of his coat.

'It's Sparticat isn't it?' he said quickly, paying no attention when I corrected him.

'I'm Fleetus and I'll be your teacher for today's session. Don't worry, we'll soon have you up to speed.'

Fleetus pointed to the far side of the enclosure and explained that today's lesson might be a bit difficult because they'd been having problems with the chariots, or 'rigs' as the drivers call them. I noticed that the fencing was all broken down on one side of the ring. Something had crashed into the fence, leaving a hole you could drive an cart through.

Fleetus asked me what experience I'd had with dogs and driving. I was afraid to say that my experiences of dogs were bad. I had been bitten seven times in my life. I explained that I have been driven, once or twice, in Master Clawdius' cart but apart from that I have little to say on the subject of roads, except that the ones in the centre of Rome are becoming very busy. High levels of traffic do seem to cause the cart drivers some irritation, as they seem to lose their tempers and begin to hiss and shout a lot.

As I spoke I could tell that Fleetus was disappointed so I stopped short of explaining my views about the Chariot Charge. Fleetus explained that his pupils usually progress to the battle chariot after spending some years working their way up through the leagues until they had a few competitive wins under their belts. He told me not to worry and said we'd better start with some road theory. He asked me if I was a fan of the chariot races. I lied and said that I went sometimes and enjoyed them.

'Hercatules be praised!' he exclaimed. 'Well, forget anything that you've heard from your friends about tactics and so on, they are all armchair drivers. Bad advice is worse than no advice at all.'

He explained the three rules of the professional charioteer, which I shall record here.

Chariot Rules

Rule I
Control your chariot at all times.

Rule II
Use your weapons accurately.

Rule III
Do not worry about things behind you.
For what is behind you cannot hurt you.

Then he picked up some leather reins and showed me how to use them to steer the dogs to the left or the right. That was the end of the first lesson.

Tomorrow I am to be introduced to the dogs and get my first practical session in a racing rig, if one can be found for me. Tonight I have been told to familiarise myself with the race circuit.

I have nothing further to add now except that Kitus has abandoned the plan about the tunnel under the Western Wall because the sandy soil there is frequently used by the guards for their toilet when they do not have time to make it back to their barracks on the east side of the school.

CATILIS IX

July 9th

Walking the Dogs

I HAVE BEEN INTRODUCED to the dogs. They are
tireless and fast but not very obedient. There were
no chariots available so I spent all morning walking
the circuit with them, pulling my reins to the left and
right to command them to make a turn. However, they
did not take much notice of my instructions.

I was wondering whether I should complain to
Fleetus about this, but it was time for lunch, so I held
my tongue. After lunch, Fleetus told me that the dogs
had complained about my driving. He said they found
it humiliating to go out with a learner driver and no
rig. After discussions we agreed that it would be best
for me to walk the circuit alone until such times as a
chariot could be found.

Whilst walking in the afternoon, I happened to
come upon an old tabby raking the sand of the circuit.
He was using a stout rake made of cedar. Remembering
Isis' words about the shortage of rakes caused by the
Fleagyptian galley going down in a storm, I hailed
him and couldn't resist complimenting him on it. He
seemed surprised at my interest.

'Please the sand with your steps my brother,' I
called with a wave. Checking to see that we weren't
being observed, I gave him a little of 'The Shifting

Dunes' pattern just to be sure he understood my meaning.

But he stared at me in wonder and began to back away.

'Wait, come back! I am your brother in the Ancient Craft of Ring Rakers,' I called.

Cornered in the far end of the enclosure, he was gasping for breath.

'I don't know who taught you to make fun of an old cleaner, but gladiator or no, I'll give you a taste of this rake if you don't leave me alone,' he hissed.

I couldn't work out what I had done to offend him but I backed away, low to the ground.

'You're wrong in the head!' he called with a shake of his rake.

I have decided to mention this to Isis, but it will have to wait until tomorrow as Fleetus has found me a rig and I must go to chariot practice.

CATILIS X

July 10th

More News from Katrin

FORTUNE BE PRAISED! At last a good spin from your wheel. Yesterday night a guard arrived with a letter for me.

Dearest Sparti,

It is your Katrin writing this note. It's good

to be able to send word to you again. Sorry about the delay but many prisoners have disappeared recently and at first we feared the worst. But I have good news. If our plan works, you shall be free before the games begin.

Your dearest Katrin.

P.S.
If our plan fails then watch for us in the crowd at the games and trust to your friend in high places. According to Cursus, your Gladiatorial School is one of the hardest to get into in the whole of Rome, so at least you are getting a good education.

CATILIS XI

July 11th

Free at Last!

ALMIGHTY MEWPITER BE PRAISED! This is the last entry of my prison diary, for as promised, a sign appeared on the message board today. Word of this spread very quickly and soon there was a large crowd standing in the yard, with the usual jostling for position. I squeezed towards the front and read:

It was as if Chaos had thrown Reason down from
Mount Olympuss. All around was the sound of hissing and jealous wails, purrs of celebration and yowls
of despair as each gladiator found out whether or not
they were on the list. As usual many disputes in the
crowd were being settled by tooth and claw. My heart
rose as I read down the list, which was not a long one.

BRUPUSS
KITERO
SCRACHUS
MOGUS

There was no Spartapuss listed. Despair set my heart
like concrete.

Then I read the following and understood Katrin's
message:

SPECIAL PARDONS FOR POISONING

All poisoners are to be released by
special order of the Emperor, in his mercy
on the occasion of the Festival of Purrcury.

Please report to the Father's office for your
poisoner's paperwork before leaving.

I am guessing now, but surely Master Clawdius must
have got this law passed at the Senate, for who else
do I know who has influence there? It is traditional
to offer a pardon to one group of criminals before
the Festival of Purrcury, who is of course the god
of thieves. When I reached the clerk's office, I was
amazed at what I saw. The crime of poisoning must be
a common one, for there was a queue of some thirty or
more of us snaking down the steps, all talking about
their favourite poisons.

It is true that the crowd was mainly made up of
yellows, but some reds and greens were there too. This
kept the guards busy, and you can imagine the talk.

'I'm Pusspero the poisoner – known for my fatal
fungi, let me through for my release!' And so on. But
it was no use. Only those of us who were listed as
poisoners were given our release papers.

I made my mark on the papers, and came back to
collect my belongings from the cell. I am not over-
joyed, for I cannot forget my poor friends here. Kitus
especially, who has treated me with such kindness.
Fortune has spun his life into a tangle. I wonder where
Isis may be found for I wish I could say goodbye.

I have cancelled my chariot lesson, perhaps it is for
the best. I wouldn't like to be the second driver in a
week to ruin one of Fleetus' precious rigs.

CATILIS XII

July 12th

Please Release Me!

THERE HAS BEEN A DELAY. I am now back in my cell awaiting instructions. But I am sure that I will be released shortly.

CATILIS XIII

July 13th

My Last Dinner

The Ides of Catilis have brought me a terrible spin. I am not free. I was stopped at the gates. I fear that someone has informed on me, for the six claws on each of my front paws were immediately noted. I was asked to provide a pedigree document to prove my breed. Of course, I do not have a pedigree certificate, so I was arrested again.

Although I have been pardoned of the charge of poisoning, I am still to participate in the games – but not as a gladiator, not even as a Fraidipuss. Tomorrow I shall make my entrance in a cage, as a wild beast.

Tonight my friends are making offerings to Hercatules, the god of the gladiators, then they will feast on their 'last meals'. You can eat as much as you want, and some go into frenzy with it, but they water down the fish sauce, apparently.

We 'beasts' do not get a last meal as we must be kept ravenous prior to our entrance into the Arena. So, instead of feasting with the rest of them, I went and sat by the steps of the training arena. With the moonlight streaming down, I thought about everyone who has ever known me.

As Isis suggested, I have left a message for Tefnut in the sand, that she may reveal herself. I have written her name backwards as instructed. Nothing has happened yet, but the night is young and the moon still high in the sky. I shall give the ring one last raking to pass the time. Kitus told me to be strong, for if the gods are willing, we shall fight well tomorrow. But I do not think he sounded very convinced. I think he read those lines from one of Dogren's leaflets.

I have decided to leave this diary to Katrin in my will, so I have to spend the rest of the night crossing out anything bad that I've said about her cooking.

CATILIS XIV

July 14th

My Diary Ends

IT IS THE MORNING of the Games of Purrcury. Perhaps this will be the final entry in my diary. Exactly why I did not get much sleep last night is a strange tale. I should love to find a cushion some where and sit in the shade while I try to make sense of it. In three hours I shall make my entrance into the Arena, through the Gate of Beasts. None who have entered through that gate have ever returned, but there is always hope. Many things have been revealed. I finally met Tefnut, amazing creature that she is and I spoke with her. What I learned, I shall set down here and so I can think about it later, if there is a later.

I wrote Tefnut's name backwards in the sand of the practice ring, just as Isis had told me. She'd said that this would only work on a moonlit night. Mewpiter himself had ordered up a marvellous moon last night and it filled the ring with light. I had not been waiting long on the stone steps when I noticed a figure bounding across the ring towards me.

'Tefnut?' I called.

I recognised Isis' laugh. She flipped something towards me: it was the coin I'd given her to buy the information.

'Isis the cleaner, Tefnut the Doctor – they are but two of my faces,' she answered.

When she said her name it sounded strange and musical: Tef-nooot.

She laughed again. But I was disappointed, this was another terrible spin. How was I to survive the Arena without proper instruction? I thought it best not to say anything, but Isis, or Tefnut as I should now call her, could read me very well.

'Are you surprised that there is more than one side to me? It is the same for all of us. Spartapuss the slave

– Spartapuss the prisoner – Spartapuss the gladiator – Spartapuss the Ring Raker...'

She laughed as she said this last one.

'But what about my lessons?' I began. 'There's no time left. I thought ...'

She interrupted me.

'You thought that Tefnut would make you a better fighter. Well, you were right. She's given you all the instruction that you'll need, at least against the opponents that you'll face tomorrow.'

'But you taught me ring raking. I am very well trained in it but I cannot see what use it will be against an armed gladiator, or a battle chariot.'

With this she leapt into the ring, twisting in one direction and reversing suddenly in a strange dance. As she passed over the letters I'd written backwards in the sand to summon her, she flicked out her tail. When the dust settled, I watched in amazement as the letters now spelt the name TEFNUT. It was as if some invisible paw had rearranged them.

'Ring raking, as you call it, is a method for fighting with spear, stick or paw. But it is the ability to control your opponent that makes it special.'

And with those words, as if to prove her point, I began to sink slowly into the sand.

'This knowledge comes to you now from kingdoms that were forgotten long ago, if they were ever known to Rome. 'As with all arts, there have been disputes and uncertainties. Disagreements in the tradition have led to differences in the patterns. Blood has been spilled over them.'

She paused for a moment and gazed up at the night sky and I noticed the brightness of the constellation Sirius, the Dog Star.

'You have mastered the first three: The Shifting Dunes, The Salt Tears, and The Bleached Bones. This pyramid supports the rest. They will serve you well tomorrow against anything this school puts against you. Even the fiercest of their fighters have the minds of newborns.'

Then she suggested that we run though my patterns one more time, as if it were the Arena tomorrow. There were many questions I wanted to ask but I gratefully accepted this chance for a final practice. Only when I had stepped through each pattern, was I allowed to exchange the wooden rake for a trident which she had brought for me. Taking a defensive stance, she beckoned me to attack. Now I began to understand. My spear questioned my opponent's every move.

'Remember what you've learned,' she said. 'Don't let anger be your master.'

'I'll try...' I began.

'And don't go trying to salute any old cleaner you see carrying a wooden rake!' she laughed.

She later explained that she'd made up everything. There was no Ancient Order of Ring Rakers. I asked her if I should still please the sand with my steps. She said that it could do no harm. Taking her leave, she padded off into the shadows.

When I returned to my cell, I noticed the coin she'd given me. On one side there was the head of the Emperor Tiberius, as on any coin, but on the other side the markings were in a language that I have never seen before. There is no time to think of this, for I must conceal my diary now and prepare myself. If Fortune spins it right, I shall start a new chapter of my diary when the fight is over. If it goes ill, I shall be dragged along the Arena floor on a hook, by a black cat in dark robes and dropped though a trapdoor. And that will be the end of Spartapuss.

I cannot think of any final words of my own, although I have tried, so I leave you with the words of the philosopher Pawralius:

> *In a little while, everything we see will have perished.*
> *We will all go down the same road. And then what difference will there be between the grandest old cat and the kitten that did not survive the winter?*

CATILIS XVII

July 17th

The Games of Purrcury

AFTER TWO EXTRAORDINARY DAYS, here I sit, in danger once more. This time the danger is that I, being thicker furred, may become cruelly overheated if I remain in the sun for too long. Then I shall be forced to bear the sudden pain of the frigidarium for a short plunge in the iced pool. And I shall need to visit the vomitorium if I eat another bowl of fish liquor. The sauces here at Bathhausia are heavier than I am used to.

I am in a garden, and not in the afterlife! Only now, am I able to tell the story of the Games of Purrcury, where I was an important but unwilling participant. The tale is full of unexpected spins and the result is better than I could have hoped for. But it is not without sadness, and I cannot turn back the clock or ask Fortune to spin again.

I will take up my tale on the morning of the Games.

Many of my fellows were sick after eating their final meal the night before, as is the tradition. Although the portions were large, little attention was paid to the quality. One of the cooks said that there were rarely any complaints afterwards.

I had been busy at my training half the night, so I had not had time for a final meal. On returning to my cell, I nibbled some dried squid that I had been saving for occasions like this. I carefully broke off a piece and put the rest back in a place of safe-keeping under the bed. Then, on second thoughts, I ate the rest in one go. Some say that we should live each day as if it is our last, but having faced death, I'd say this is probably a bad idea because we'd make ourselves thoroughly sick.

Shortly after sunrise, we arrived at the Games. The journey had not taken long, as there is a private road between the school and the Arena. It helps to keep the crowds away from the star gladiators. When we arrived at the gates, the Imperial colours were flying and the guards were in good humour, waving us on without raising their whips. I didn't see any branding irons either, but perhaps they were still heating them up.

I got my first glimpse inside the Arena through a crack in the wall. It was already about half full. A flight of gulls rose to the roof, turning circles above the fish sellers who were making a mess as usual.

The ring itself was shaped like a half moon and very like our training area, save for a grand stage that had been set up in the middle, opposite the Imperial box. On the stage there was a poor copy of a triumphal arch and the statue of Tiberius, which was leaning to the left.

The musicians had just finished tuning up. They launched into a number called 'Slay, Slay, Slay for the Glory of Caesar!' and a couple of clowns ran into the centre of the ring and started to play-fight. The crowd's reaction was mixed. Some clapped and beat their seats in time whilst others wore the weary expressions of wolves that had been served up a salad.

The Arena was filling up fast. Soon the stands would be packed full of Rome's noblest felines and lowest strays. The Senators sat cool in the shade of the upper levels whilst the mob baked in the heat near the sand. Already they were fighting over their places with more relish than some of my fellow gladiators would fight for their lives. The yellows especially, who had made the most of their last meal, looked as fat as barrels. Too fat to do much running!

The Imperial box was still empty, the tradition being that the most honoured guests are last to take their places before the show. Thinking of my friends, I searched the front rows for familiar faces, but I couldn't see any. I wondered if I would have come to watch them die, if the Fortune had spun things differently.

A noise dragged my attention back to a guard, who was checking names against a list of equipment. Costumes and armour were being given out. Whilst many of us were worried about our lives, I was surprised at the amount of excitement, particularly amongst the reds and greens, at the prospect of wearing the new costumes and fighting with the real weapons. As it turned out, we weren't given our swords or tridents until immediately before our fights, but the guards were already giving out shields and helmets. Puman's red team could not believe it when they picked up their square shields. They were half the weight of those used for practice. There was a certain pride about these reds, in their body movements, as if they knew they had been well trained. If Doctor Puman was watching, he'd be satisfied with his work. Likewise Dogren's greens looked suitably fierce as they brandished their shields. Their helmets had been polished till they reflected the blinding sun.

When all the costumes had been given out, a guard announced an order for all 'beasts' to make their way to their cages. As I was now classified as a wild animal rather than a gladiator, I was to be unleashed into the Arena via the Gate of Beasts. (This is usually a dramatic moment in the games as the fearless gladiator faces the gate, waiting for the release of who knows what terror.) Due to the shortage of real beasts in today's performance, some make-up artists had been employed. They said they were aiming to give me a wilder look by painting me with tiger stripes and giving me a good coating of red paint to make my jaws look blood-soaked. The idea was to make me seem as savage and menacing as possible. No mirror was available for me to see the results for myself. When the assistants were happy, I left the make up area. Just as I was entering my holding cage, I was distracted by a low hiss. A guard pushed a note under the wooden bars, which were for show and could never have held a wild animal. I read it quickly.

OFFICIAL PROGRAMME

The Games of Purrcury

I.   *Opening Ceremony*
II.   *The Parade of the Gladiators*
III. *Distribution of Fish, Wine and Milk*
IV.   *Games: Part One*
V.   *Wild Beast v Imperial Charioteer*
VI.   *Lunchtime Executions*
VII. *Plus: 'A Theatrical Spectacle'*
VIII. *Games: Part Two*
IX.   *Closing Ceremony*

I Scratchus, have written this notice, in association with Bathhausia, Rome's best Purrmanian Bath House.

May I warn the reader against believing the claims of Bathhausia, for I know for a fact that they still have a problem with an algal bloom in their main bathing pool, that has turned the water green. The cause of this has baffled Rome's finest minds, although it has been said that the customers are doing something in the water that is forbidden. I was about to discard this programme when I turned it over and saw this note.

Dearest Sparti,

It is your Katrin here. We heard that you have been arrested again. Fear not, for we are still working for your release. We have written to the Emperor Tiberius to ask him to make you an honorary pedigree certificate. We hope that he will grant this on account of your many years of service to Rome. Cursus also told me to mention that you are the only one who knows how to work the controls of the Spatopia central heating system. Only by your release can we guarantee hot water for the Imperial baths at any time of the day, is how he put it.

Which brings me to a personal matter: whilst trying to discover how to work the heating, Cursus discovered your secret diary, which you had concealed behind a waste water overflow pipe. Fear not, for we promise not to read it any more than is absolutely necessary. I have granted Cursus a quick glance in order to find the plans indicating the heating controls. I must leave you now but we will come to visit you backstage if Cleocatra can get us tickets. I hope that this letter has reached you in time. I had Cursus carve a prayer for your safety onto my best dinner bowl

and I threw it into the Sacred Spring for
the goddess. May she give you the strength
of a lion!

I confess that this letter disturbed me. For one thing, my friends had now read my secret diary. I wish I'd carried on writing it in Kittish! Secondly, there had been talk and betting in the spa on my performance at the games. My friends were eagerly awaiting my entrance as a proud gladiator, not as a ravening animal with red lips and an imitation mane made out of straw. I felt something I do not normally feel, I think it was shame! I was also afraid. Imperial pardons are rare and it's a long way from Rome to the island of Capri. Would the Emperor's reply reach me in time? Come to think of it, I had never heard of an emperor pardoning a wild beast before. How I wished to be a Fraidipuss! At least they had their nets and tridents. But the yellows were all feeling worse than I did. How they wished that they were reds or especially greens (as this was Catligula's favoured team and they were expected to win everything). But for all of our wishing, the games were about to begin.

The fanfare sounded. All eyes were on the Imperial box. The guests of honour were taking their places on their ceremonial cushions. The Patron of the Games was almost ready to begin his speech. Not everyone fell quiet immediately as bets were still being placed, free dormouse kebabs were being given out

133

and there were arguments about who could have seconds. Eventually shouts of 'Silence!', went around the auditorium, from the Imperial bodyguard and the Spraetorians. These shouts made it even harder to hear the opening speeches.

'Welcome friends, Romans and strays to Purrcury's Games, given in honour of my favourite nephew. He becomes a fully-grown cat this year. May he bring great honour to Rome, like his dear father before him.'

I didn't recognise the voice, but I knew the face. It was Master Clawdius. Reclining on a purple cushion to his right was Mewlia. Seated on his left was another female. I didn't recognise her at the time, in fact I almost took her for a tomcat, due to her heavy features and big build. I later learned that her name was Mogullania. Her amber eyes never left Clawdius once during the opening speech, which he read from a scroll. The actor Napellus stood next to him and repeated each line, in his loudest theatrical voice.

Clawdius said a lot of nice things about Catligula. Those of us who know Clawdius well were a little surprised, for he had once called his nephew: 'The most spoilt kitten in all of Rome'.

Catligula, for his part, had little love for his uncle. After his father, Purrmanipuss, had died on campaign, the young Catligula had been brought up by Mewlia and the Emperor Tiberius. It is said that these two could not understand how one so feeble and nervous as Clawdius could be any relation of theirs. Catligula copied his grandparents' example and teased his uncle mercilessly.

Catligula sharpened his claws with a file as Clawdius read lie after lie about his good character from the scroll. 'Kind', 'loyal', 'helpful', 'hard working', 'the servant of Rome' and so on. I wondered who had come up with this list of good points. Probably Mewlia's scribes. Surely Clawdius couldn't have written this himself? There was open laughter in some parts of the crowd. Although they may have been laughing at the effect of the actor Napellus repeating Clawdius' words in his best voice. It sounded like an echo that was louder than the original.

Soon Clawdius moved on to thank Mewlia and Tiberius. As he praised the great Emperor, the actor Napellus gestured dramatically towards the mighty golden statue that towered over the west side of the Arena. As I looked up at Tibbles' statue, I remembered Katrin's plan to get me an Imperial pardon. It was too late! The trumpets were sounding, the games were beginning.

Clawdius invited the guest of honour to take his place upon the ceremonial cushion. Catligula took an age to settle. Whilst he circled on the seat, Clawdius shook with nerves. The band launched into a quick chorus of 'Purr if You Like Catligula' to hurry things on.

In his capacity as Patron of the Games, Clawdius gave word to light the torch that would signal the start of the parade. The crowd was calling for us already. They say that nothing can prepare a new gladiator for the experience of walking through the Gate of Death for the first time. I was entering via the Beasts' Gate and certainly nothing had prepared me for the shame of being paraded around the Arena in a cage, with instructions to roar whenever approached. As the crowd spotted their favourite gladiators they greeted them with adoring mews. When a fighter they did not favour passed, they let out a wall of wails and hisses that could be heard all the way to the shores of the Tiber. Thankfully they parked my cage after half a circuit of the Arena when a wheel fell off, so I did not need to make a full circuit.

As the gladiators paraded in their costumes, those who were going to fight first were already warming up in the centre of the Arena. The crowd purred in appreciation as one Furasian, something of an exhibitionist, sent her round shield spinning high into the air and then caught it with one outstretched paw. Meanwhile bets were being placed. Clawdius had already inspected the weapons. With large sums in gold at stake, it was not unheard of for a poisoned blade to be used to help Fortune do her work.

As is the tradition, we professionals were joined for the warm-up by certain enthusiastic amateurs. It has been quite the fashion in Rome recently to take part in the games. One of these was trading blocks and blows with Katus. My friend's eyes searched the Arena for his brother Kitus as he sparred with his amateur opponent. Kitus was limbering up nearby, crouched low to the ground. He looked frightened. The crowd laughed when the amateur failed to block a light blow from Katus' wooden sword. He let out a mew of pain and collapsed as if fatally wounded. A moment later he sprang up, backed away, and inspected his tail for damage. Unscratched, he took up his gladius again as the crowd hissed him.

The band struck up with a famous tune called *Walk Slowly Now, for Death Approaches!* It got faster and faster, despite the title. I recognised the tuba player whom we'd hired for the Imperial visit back at Spatopia. He'd put on weight: the band specialised in funerals and there had been a lot of them recently!

Purrcury and Cha-ron, who were bringing up the rear of the parade, had almost made a complete circuit now. Cha-ron, the Lord of the Underworld, was cloaked, wore a tall hood, and carried an enormous metal hook. The effect would have been more dramatic if he hadn't kept tripping over. Luckily Purrcury, the god of thieves, was there to help hold him up. These two worked as a team during the games, with Cha-ron pulling the defeated gladiator through the Gate of Death with his hook, but not before Purrcury had poked them a few times with a red hot iron to make sure that they weren't pretending to be dead.

In vain I scanned the front seats for Katrin or any familiar face. Then I was distracted by a crash from the centre of the Arena. An assistant was throwing pine logs towards a heavily armoured figure seated on a chariot. The gladiator hacked at the logs and split them into tiny pieces with a double-bladed axe before they fell to the sand. I remember my dismay at this sight. It was Brutia! She growled at the crowd as a rain of splinters fell all over the place. At least the end would be brief!

At last the parade ended and the gladiators left the Arena. The next time they entered the ring would be for real. There was a crash on the cymbal and the crowd fell silent.

'Let the Games begin!' cried Clawdius.

At this, a furious Purrcury waved his branding iron at the front row. They were howling with laughter because Clawdius had forgotten his lines.

'Er, in the name of Purrcury, let the Games begin,' said Clawdius apologetically. Mewlia rolled her eyes as if she had been expecting this sort of mistake for quite some time.

Then I noticed a disturbance at the back of the Imperial box, a messenger had arrived and was making his way towards Clawdius with a scroll in his paw. I admit that the thought of the pardon now crossed my mind. But it could have been a thousand other messages... greetings from the holiday isle of Capri perhaps.

There was a sharp clang of metal on metal as the blade of a sword hit the prongs of a trident. Why was

I thinking about my own rescue? Poor Kitus was fighting for his life. Kitus and Katus stood a tail's length apart from each other in the centre of the Arena. Kitus, being a yellow, was equipped with a net in his left paw and a trident in his right. Not that either was likely to prove useful. He'd told me that he had not been training since he'd heard he had to fight his brother. Now the moment had arrived, he stood stock still. The move to block the sword thrust was purely instinctive, as if some invisible paw had guided his spear across to defend his face. Should he stand and wait for death, or raise his claws against his own brother?

'Hit him! Don't tickle him! What are you waiting for?' shouted the crowd.

Here was a mismatch if ever I'd seen one. You could tell by their markings that they'd come from the same litter but Katus was twice his size. Now there would be no rest till one of them was dragged dead through the sand on the end of Cha-ron's hook. Death would be needed to satisfy the crowd. Not that they seemed to be enjoying themselves much. The delay drew hisses from all across the Arena and shouted insults. Why didn't they get on with the bout? There were calls for the Spraetorian guard. Purrcury got his hot iron ready just in case the gladiators refused to fight.

At last Katus struck a blow with his sword, trying to kill time rather than his brother. Kitus parried, but less effectively this time, as his brother's sword glanced off the point of his trident and grazed his flank. As he leapt to the left, drops of crimson stained the sand. The crowd cheered their approval. Some of them had their claws unsheathed, as if they themselves had drawn the blood of an enemy. Kitus rolled leftwards, regained his balance and raced towards the Gate of Death. The crowd spat and hissed, proving their ignorance. Running away and tiring the enemy out is a good tactic for a Fraidipuss. Who would want to trade blows at close range without the protection of armour or a shield?

Katus hissed back at the crowd, waving his sword in the faces of the front rows. He approached his brother cautiously as if to pounce. Then the two of them ran at each other at full speed.

Katus was charging at Kitus, in the way that the Purmillo had been taught. Kitus stood perfectly still, his eyes half closed. He was prepared to meet his ancestors without dishonour. But, at the last moment, Katus sidestepped his brother and he crashed directly through the Gate of Death, knocking the hook from Cha-ron's paws as he disappeared backstage. The crowd went wild. Several fights broke out between those who had bet on the net cat to win and were now due a tidy profit. Kitus sat motionless on the sidelines, as the Arena boiled like a pot of hot fish liquor.

A company of Spraetorians raced backstage after Katus. The crowd had seen this sort of thing before and fully expected him to be brought back under armed escort. The tradition then was that Clawdius, the Patron of the Games, should decide whether or not he had fought bravely and could live. There was little hope of this in this case since running away was against the rules. The Purmillo hung their heads and crouched low to the ground. Katus had fled from combat and, in doing so, he had brought dishonour to the whole red team. We waited for some time but still there was no sign of Katus. Had the guards lost him backstage?

Clawdius looked worried. There were hisses as he rose from his cushion. The actor Nappellus stood behind him, once again ready to repeat his words in a stronger voice. There was little space in the Imperial box and one of the attendants nudged Clawdius accidentally with his tail, causing him to wobble for a moment. Small trickles of foam formed around his mouth. I noticed Mewlia looking at Clawdius in disgust and then at the statues of the Imperial family. Perhaps she was thinking that Clawdius' brother Purrmanipuss was brilliant with crowds and would never have allowed this festival to turn into such a shambles.

From where I was sitting, the situation looked as if it could go either way. Riots were not unknown at such events and now the Imperial bodyguards were standing ready. Clawdius seemed at a loss about what to do. The obvious thing would be to send the next pair of gladiators in and have done with it. I later learned that Katus' unexpected exit had created a problem for Clawdius, who was in charge of events. It was widely known that Mewlia was fiercely traditional. To continue the sport whilst an armed gladiator was on the run was not in the rule book and would set tongues wagging and tails flicking. Clawdius was far more terrified of his grandmother than he was of breaking traditions, but a decision had to be made.

Mogullania whispered something in Clawdius' ear and then leant over to Catligula on his cushion. A few words were exchanged. Then the slaves started to distribute bucketsful of iced fish to the crowd. If they couldn't have blood, free fish would have to do!

Finally, Clawdius rose to address the crowd. There were shouts again for silence. Then Clawdius began:

'Soon my friends the Games of Purrcury will continue.'

There were cheers, hurrahs and a few hisses.

'But not before you have had some more entertainment...'

Shouts of 'Yes!'

'...of a theatrical nature.'

Gasps and shouts of 'No. No!'

'I give you Nappellus, a mighty actor, whose fame is known throughout the world. Or at least throughout all Rome, which is the centre of the world ...'

Mews of approval.

'And appearing with him, a newcomer to the stage, in a play that he has rewritten himself from the ancient texts...'

Silence. The crowd knew it made sense to be cautious on occasions like this and they were proved right.

'Please welcome the son of my dear brother Purrmanipuss...'

Huge applause. How they loved Purrmanipuss!

'...our guest of honour, who comes of age this year, has written this play himself.'

Calls of 'Catligula! Catligula!' Someone then could not resist adding 'He's such a lovely figula!' as they insist on doing at these occasions.

'So now, let the play begin!'

With a graceful bound, Nappellus leapt onto the stage, which had been set up directly opposite the Imperial box. Some carpenters were still putting the finishing touches to the scenery. The performance had been scheduled for lunchtime, after the executions of the criminals, but the crew was an experienced bunch and were making short work of rigging this quickly. A great rock with a chain and an iron collar attached to it was swung into position. Opposite this was an enormous golden throne. The carpenters scampered off and the actors were ready.

Nappellus, who was the narrator, stood at the front of the stage. Onto the throne leapt Catligula. He was also masked and with his coat now completely whitened by the best in theatrical make up (a powder that was used to bleach carpets). He carried a lightening bolt, representing Peus, the most powerful Squeak god, who we Romans would call Mewpiter. The crowd cheered as he took his place. Then Nappellus began in his marvellous voice:

Silence please and you'll hear me speak,
A tale in the tongue of the ancient Squeaks,
A dreadful tale of the goddess Fate,
If you don't speak Squeak, then I can translate.

Almighty Peus on Mount Olympuss sat,
God of the gods, and of dogs and cats.
An angry lord on a golden mat,
Something must have upset him,
With a face like that!

This unusual start to the performance made some sections of the crowd laugh. The senators, who were educated and had all studied poetry, couldn't believe what they were hearing. Who had ever heard of poetry that rhymed? It just wasn't classical!

It was all terribly embarrassing. The crowds weren't taking it seriously either. They were grinning at the frightening spectacle of Catligula with his white coat. The make-up artists had powdered him so much that there were great explosions of white dust every time he changed position on stage. Trying to be professional, Catligula glowered at the audience. He loved acting and he specialised in anger. He used to practice his terrible expressions in front of the mirror. He was serious about his performances and the crowd had better be too.

'What? Am I not god-like? You'd better worship me now, or you'll regret it!' called the mighty Peus to an oyster seller in the front row, who was quivering with laughter as another puff of white powder exploded.

After a pause, Catligula read from his scroll:

Someone has stolen a secret from me,
His name is Promethypuss and you'll soon see,
justice will come to this thief and liar,
Who stole my secret - how to make fire.

Catligula gave the attendants a cue and a great rock was wheeled onto the stage. Tied to it was a prisoner in an orange collar. For a horrible moment, I thought it was Katus, but it was some other unfortunate soul.

'Read!' commanded Catligula. And the chained prisoner began:

I am Promethypuss and yes I admit it,
The crime of theft, I have committed.
I stole your fire and thus have let loose,
The secret gift of almighty Peus.
But I gave it to the kittens, so they could be warm,
For their pads get chilly in the winter's storm.
And the cold at night when the white snow falls,
Gets right up their coats and into their paws.

There were hisses and mocking laughter from the crowd. Catligula pointed his thunderbolt. Another puff of white powder erupted and the crowd laughed again. Nappellus continued:

Promethypuss in fear did start to quiver,
As almighty Peus' judgement
was delivered ...

Catligula broke in:

Those snivelling kittens can stand there and shiver.
Be thankful I don't have them drowned in the river.
And I've never been known as a good forgiver,
So I'm sending an eagle
to eat your liver!

With that, the stage assistants brought forth a huge eagle. This was not a theatrical effect but a real bird of prey, which they tied to Promethypuss' rock by means of a long leather cord. The crowd gazed in awe at the mighty bird. Even the most hardened of critics amongst them agreed that this effect was rather good.

The eagle flapped its great wings as the stage assistants tried to poke it off its perch with their wooden poles. Finally the bird of prey swooped down and settled. It was twice the size of the rock.

As the bird eyed the prisoner mercilessly, the crowd gasped and applauded. The theatre was finally working its magic! Catligula admired the scene, waving and pointing with his thunderbolt. The eagle flapped with great force but, try as it might, it could not escape from the leather cord that bound it fast to earth.

Promethypuss shouted his protests. He had done nothing to deserve this. He was not Promethypuss, he was not even an actor, he was a fishmonger's apprentice who had run away from his master's shop and been arrested. His cries were silenced as the eagle's mighty talon struck towards his head with all the force of a stone mason's chisel. The crowd cheered wildly, driving the great bird madder and madder. Flapping with all its might, it broke free from its ropes and was now face to face with Nappellus. There was another great crack and Rome's finest actor lost his head.

Far from being angry at this unplanned departure from his script, Catligula was delighted. Three times the mighty bird flapped towards him and three times he beat it away with nothing more than made up verses and fierce looks. In the excitement, he'd dropped his scroll but he continued with the performance by improvising. Still in character, he waved a paw and addressed the crowd, begging them:

'Wait! Wait! Don't mourn him yet. His head will grow back at sunrise if I, Peus command it.'

The bird of prey had broken completely free now and the audience was in terror as the Imperial bodyguards rushed Catligula from the stage. The crowd hissed and spat. They were outraged at this disgraceful performance. They had been pleased with the execution of the prisoner, which had been cleverly done, but Nappellus was Rome's favourite actor. He was loved throughout the civilised world.

'Who is responsible?' they screamed.

At this moment, I must have been one of the few cats in the crowd whose eyes were on the Imperial box rather than the spectacle on stage. It had not been a good day at the theatre for Clawdius. I wondered what he was thinking. He was the Patron of these Games, would he be punished for this embarrassment? First one of his gladiators escapes, and now a killer bird of prey goes on the loose.

The eagle had now flapped into the middle of the ring and twenty Spraetorian guards struggled to catch it with a net. They were backed up by Purrcury, who had heated up his branding iron and was lunging at the tail of the great bird. But the eagle had no intention of being captured. Escaping from its ties, it took to the sky, where it must have had a great view of the carnage below. Now it had its freedom and it could go wherever it pleased.

But I did not have long to think of this, because a paw shook my cage and a voice said:

'Get ready Spartapuss. You're on.'

Clawdius stood up and addressed the crowd as best he could.

'Noble Senators, citizens, Romans, hear me now. I know that things have not gone well so far.'

Mewlia rolled her eyes to the heavens once more, for members of the Imperial family never say they are sorry.

'But, if Mewpiter wills it, our second half will make good the errors of our first. For now, in a change to the advertised order, we present a thrilling display of skill and feline mastery over canine and machine.

Now a fearless bestiari will chase a ravenous animal in a chariot. Let the wild beast hunt begin!'

Purrcury waved his fist furiously at the Imperial box and brandished his poker.

'Er, I mean, in Purcurry's name, let the hunt begin!' added Clawdius.

As they made ready with the winch, to swing my cage into the area behind the Gate of Beasts for my entrance, I heard a spectator at the front moaning

'Boring old chariots. What's the point of them? They just go round and round and round?'

I couldn't disagree with this.

Another voice added: 'This is typical of the imperials. I came here for some gladiators and they're showing us dog-carts.'

These two didn't seem impressed with Clawdius' promise of a spectacular attack by a dangerous wild beast. By now it was known throughout all Rome that the real wild beasts had hoofed it the moment that the Games had been announced. The crowd still wanted their blood sports but, from where I was swinging, there didn't seem to be a lot of sport in this. A trained charioteer, in a heavily armed rig drawn by a team of hounds, against me? Unlike real beasts, I was armed only with heavy make-up and a straw mane that kept slipping down.

The charioteer would make a few circuits of the ring and soften me up with a couple of arrows. Then he'd leap down and put an end to me with his gladius as the band played Slay, Slay, Slay for the Glory of Rome. It would all be over before they reached the second verse!

As the cage swung from side to side on the crane I had a great view of the Arena, where my executioner was waiting. The charioteer drove the battle chariot into the ring. Four enormous hounds pulled the rig. Once they were clear of the attendants, they began to pick up their pace. They were race-bred dogs and would not get into their stride until a lap or two had been completed. The band struck up with the chariots theme. When my cage was in place they made ready to open the Gate of Beasts. I heard a command from the Imperial box.

'Unleash the beast!'

There was slow applause.

The gate started to swing forth, but got stuck.

The opening of a gate can take an eternity when your survival hinges on what might charge at you from the other side. After what seemed like an age, they decided that they could not shift it, so I was ordered back into the cage to be winched into the Arena. The crane swung me over the wall, an attendant pulled a cord and the bottom of my cage flew open. I twisted around and righted myself rather neatly in mid fall.

I landed paws down on the sand with considerable force.

The charioteer raised the visor, saluted the Imperial guests and finally turned to face me. Brutia's eyes met mine.

Perhaps she'd dreamed of this revenge all throughout our imprisonment together, but it was now too late to wonder what I'd done to make her dislike me so much. Not waiting for me to make a move, Brutia urged the team forward towards me, she meant to run me down, and her team was trained to run all day. For encouragement's sake she gave the dogs a stroke of the whip (the only type of stroke she knew).

I took off like Purrcury himself! I was running from instinct for there was no cover to be found in the wide expanse of the sand. I could feel drool from the jaws of the hounds at my tail as they snapped in pursuit. In the centre of the ring stood a wooden post with spinning blades. It was a device of the same type that I had seen the Purmillo use in training. The blades whirled round and round like steel windmills. But I headed straight for the confusion of the whirring blades, where I hoped that the dogs would fear to follow.

As I ran headlong towards the machine, I knew that I must make a last minute leap to avoid the blades. Should I jump to the left or to the right? I decided to ask Fortune which way to leap for, although she may be blind, it is never said that Fortune cannot answer a simple question when it is put to her.

'Left,' I heard her whisper. Waiting till the last moment, I hurled myself leftwards with all my force. But in mid spring, I heard another voice answer me. It was Tefnut's.

'To the right Spartapuss, leap to the right if you would not join your ancestors.'

Without thinking, I changed my mind and leapt rightwards. But I lost my balance and found myself sliding straight towards the machine. By some spin from Fortune, I flew straight through its whizzing blades and ended up behind the wooden post. The hounds were almost upon me but now they had a problem. The lead dogs saw my leap too late. They didn't know whether or not to follow me. Chaos drove the rig now and it slid out of control with Brutia barking curses. As the chariot skidded on a collision course, the team pulled to the right, trying to avoid the purring blades. Their last lunge was just powerful enough to heave themselves clear but the chariot overturned, skidded sideways and smashed into the great machine with a clang that brought its spinning mechanism to a halt.

From the smashed remains of the chariot, a familiar figure emerged. Brutia hadn't given up. Now that the blades no longer turned, she'd try to flush me out of my hiding place behind the jammed mechanism. A fiery arrow shot past my mane and slammed into the wooden post behind me. More burning arrows followed, making a neat cluster. The crowd, who had been cursing the charioteer for making such a mess of the hunt, now applauded her loudly and roared their approval. The wooden post had been soaked in tar. Either by happy coincidence or clever design, it was the very type of post used for burning the criminals to death during the lunchtime executions. Unlike those unfortunates, I was not wrapped up tight in a 'coat of pitch' and bound to the stake with ropes. The black smoke billowed as the tar-soaked wood caught alight and began to crackle. I had no choice but to flee from the safety of my hiding place.

I backed away from the fire wondering what to do next. The crowd was quickly onto me and shouted at the charioteer to get in for the kill. Brutia didn't seem to need their encouragement. The moment I left my hiding place she charged at me at full speed. There was nothing else to do but run. I knew that this was the worst thing I could do, for if you run from a dog, it will always give chase.

I tried to remember Tefnut's words about pleasing the sand with your steps. No, she'd made that bit up. In my terror, I'd forgotten everything.

Brutia caught up with me in front of the Imperial box. Clawdius avoided my gaze. Only he could stop this now. The crowd screamed for Brutia to finish the kill, some shouted for me to at least make a better end of it, and try to fight her paw to paw. Brutia raised her bow. It had an arrow already strung. She was about to slay me right in front of Clawdius and her mistress

Mewlia, when a voice cried:

'Wait Clawdius!'

The crowd hissed.

'Master Clawdius, this is a mistake. Don't you recognise your own servant by his six claws?'

It was Katrin.

I tore away the charred remains of my straw mane. The crowed hissed and spat, outraged at the delay. Katrin thrust a bundle of scrolls under Clawdius' nose. One of them carried the seal of the Pedigree Office.

Clawdius opened his mouth as if to speak. Words formed but no sound came out, except a little splutter. Then he began to choke as if a fur ball had got stuck in his throat.

Mewlia looked on in disgust as Catligula rose from his seat laughing.

'My dear uncle Claw seems to have swallowed something he shouldn't have. He's quite beside himself. Shall I take over, great grandmother?'

Mewlia remained silent. She was sickened by Clawdius' disgraceful performance in front of the public. Now Catligula addressed the crowd.

'Romans, hiss if this beast shall die or cheer if he shall live!'

'He's not a beast! He's Spartapuss!' cried Katrin, but her protest was lost in the uproar.

Catligula gestured to the crowd with an outstretched paw, to make their feelings known. He extended and retracted the claws on his right paw. Claws out was the signal for death. The crowd hissed like a nest of vipers and extended their claws.

I was not surprised. Arena crowds are not known to be forgiving and it had been a thin day for sport so far. Savouring the moment, Catligula pretended he could not see them, drawing up his paw to shade his eyes from the sun's glare and asking:

'What is that Romans? Do you mean life or death?'

Again he addressed Mewlia, pretending to consult with her.

'You are wise, great grandmother, what would you have me do?'

The crowd cheered and chanted Mewlia's name. A good deal of hissing continued. Mewlia bristled in anger, it was rare for her to reveal her true feelings in public.

'Stop this Gattus. You must stop this now,' she ordered. But Catligula was drunk on the attention of a thousand pairs of eyes. He was not listening.

My eyes were on Brutia. Her gaze had never left Mewlia throughout Catligula's little performance. As she stared at her former mistress, I could see all manner of things in her looks: devotion with fear, obedience with rage.

She drew back the bow and fired directly at my face. I leapt sideways and the arrow hissed past my right ear. The Arena gasped and fell silent. Brutia made ready with another arrow. Catligula screamed at her to stop, incensed by her disobedience. He ordered the guards to seize her. But, after throwing down her weapon, she leapt straight for my throat.

I hadn't expected this sudden attack and it was all I could do to keep away from Brutia's snapping jaws. As she searched for my throat, I sank my claws into her back and she dropped me like a stick. As I backed off I heard a voice shouting my name. Katrin grabbed a trident from a Fraidipuss (who was easily disarmed) and threw it to me. In doing so, she probably saved my life. Now I could put some distance between myself and my attacker. Enraged, Brutia snapped at the trident. I backed away further, unaware of the jeers of the crowd, who were at last about to get the sort of entertainment they'd been promised. Without thinking, I dodged backwards, with the same stop start motion that had seemed so strange when I first witnessed Isis perform it.

Again, Brutia snapped at the shaft of my trident, trying to wrestle it away so that she could close in for the kill. Stepping through the pattern, I danced backwards and stumbled as if to fall. Eager to take advantage of this mistake, Brutia sprang forward to attack, but her fangs missed me as I rolled away, emerging with the trident in the other paw. The 'Shifting Dunes' had worked and I was lost to her in an arc of dust and sand.

However Brutia was not yet beaten and she charged forward to find me. Though blinded by the dust, she could track me by scent alone and put an end to the chase. But she wasn't expecting my next move. I fell into another pattern, beating a rhythm on the ground with the trident.

As the dust cleared, Brutia watched in amazement. The ship of my mind had slipped its moorings. The shouts of the crowd were lost as I heard only cymbals and drums. The 'Bleached Bones' had worked its magic. A few steps away from me Brutia sank slowly below the sand until she was held fast. As she struggled, she sank deeper, until she was buried up to the very tip of her snout. The crowd, who had been hissing for my blood just minutes earlier, now cheered wildly. 'Spa-ta-puss! Spa-ta-puss!' came the chant.

Dropping the trident, I approached the Imperial platform.

'Who do they call for?' asked Mewlia.

'S-spartapuss, my slave,' said Clawdius, still choking on his words. Then Catligula spoke to me, although his words were aimed at the crowd.

'Spartapuss you have fought bravely. You have pleased us. So now I shall confer upon you, a fitting gift for bravery. A gift beyond price. Your freedom!'

As the fanfare sounded, the Arena erupted with cheers. The crowd leapt off their seats and flung their cushions into the air.

Catligula placed a wooden collar around my neck, the symbol of my freedom. Mewlia and Clawdius sat in silence. Clawdius scowled at Catligula. For one thing, as Patron of the Games, he should have been doing the freeing. For another, by law I belonged to him and I might have been valuable as a gladiator. Seeing the look that Clawdius gave him, Catligula smiled and motioned to the crowd for quiet.

Catligula addressed the crowd again.

'Romans! Hear me! As well as his freedom, my generous uncle Clawdius has just told me that this gladiator will leave the Arena today with a purse of five hundred in gold!'

'Spa-ta-puss! Spa-ta-puss!' chanted the crowd. Clawdius avoided my eyes. The guards dug Brutia out of her hole and Cha-ron dragged her through his gate with a hook.

For my part I wish that the goddess Fortune, who had already been busy that morning, had seen fit to end the story here. But the festival of Purrcury has become notorious. Not for the events that I've described so far: a runaway Purmillo, the death of an actor, a crashed chariot, a slave turned prisoner, then turned gladiator, then turned wild beast who won his freedom. So far, it had been a typical day at the Games. But no one could have predicted what was still in store that afternoon.

Saucus says that it was a pawtent that the great eagle should stop Catligula's play. Remember that three times the eagle turned away from Catligula during the attack. But Catligula was left unharmed whilst all who stood around him were carried away. Perhaps the gods have plans for him!

After my freedom was granted, Clawdius told the

guards to give the signal for lunch.

He left the platform with Mogullania following just two tails behind him. The band stood up to play the lunch theme but Catligula leapt off his cushion and commanded them to stop. He approached Mewlia and whispered in her ear. I do not know what he said. Perhaps he told her it was too early for lunch and that the crowd hadn't had any good sport yet.

Whatever the reason, he announced that he was going to give a demonstration of his skill in the Battle Chariot. He was determined to show the crowd how it was really done.

Mewlia looked horrified. Catligula raised his voice:

'Let us give them a show, great grandmother. Such a show as my father Purrmanipuss would have given.

But Mewlia reminded him of the law that no one except the Patron of the Games, or the Emperor himself could add an event to the programme. And Tiberius was Emperor, in case he had forgotten.

Catligula sneered and made some reply that I did not catch. Mewlia swiped him heavily about the ear.

'Gattus Tiberius, you will stop this!' she shouted. But it was no use. In vain Mewlia looked about for Clawdius to prevent this next humiliation, but the idiot had already shuffled off the platform for his lunch.

When Catligula made his first entrance into the Arena as a charioteer, it was in heroic fashion. Fleetus had prepared a golden chariot, pulled by a team of six huge white hounds. They didn't need to be whipped to start them off running, but Catligula gave them a taste of the lash anyway, for the sake of the crowd. He wore a palm leaf crown as if it this was a triumph in his honour, rather than a lunchtime chariot racing demonstration. He'd brought along part of his costume from the fateful play and he waived his painted thunderbolt at the crowd as he charged around the ring. There were various other theatrical touches. A torch behind the cab billowed black smoke out behind him. The sun glittered against the wheel spikes, which were hugely oversized, as was the fashion with the young drivers.

The Arena was still three quarters full when Catligula made his first lap. But many were leaving, and their minds were on roasted dormouse with garlic. Only the die-hards and disciplinarians liked to sit in the baking Arena during the lunchtime executions. The band played a dramatic theme and Catligula waved his thunderbolt, but still the majority of the crowd continued to stream towards the exits.

Catligula tried everything to win them over. He charged round and round the ring going faster and faster. In one pass he even drove a half circuit without holding the reins and then made as if to leap onto the back of one of the hounds in the manner of a circus driver. All of this to win the adoration of the crowd. But nobody was watching. Exasperated, he cast away his thunderbolt and, with a flourish that almost lost him his balance, he threw the covers away from a weapon that was mounted on the front of his chariot. I'd never seen the like of it before, but I am told it is a smaller version of the ballista that is used to shoot burning spears over the wall, when our legions have an enemy city under siege.

Slowing his dogs to a trot, he set light to the missile and took aim. With a jolt, a flaming javelin shot towards the western side of the Arena. Here the crowd was thickest, as everyone was pressing towards the exit for their free food. Whether by accident or design, Catligula's aim was high. The missile arced over the heads of the crowd. It hung in the air for what seemed like an age before crashing into the left eye of the statue of the Emperor Tiberius.

It could not have been a more accurate shot if it was fired from the bow of the war god Paws himself! For a moment the great statue rocked upon its plinth and there was a cry to clear the way in case it fell, but the crowd just stood as still as statues. The golden head of Tibbles was weeping tears of flame.

For when they said 'the statue must be made of solid gold' in the Senate, they did so without any knowledge of the craft of statue building. Look inside the heads of the statues of our emperors and gods in Rome and you will find them all full of air. Their great heads must be hollowed out so that their bodies can bear the weight of the gold plate. In the case of Tibbles' statue, the neck had been made out of straw mats, tied together with cord. Only a thin layer of gold upon the outside of the statue made it gleam.

The crowd weren't experts in the art of statue making either. They stopped in their tracks and gaped, sick with fear and horror at this sight. What could save them from Tiberius' fiery tears? Smoke bellowed from his mouth and his golden whiskers were lit up like candles. The crowd climbed the great walls in terror. Some wailed that was a pawtent about the death of their dear Emperor.

Catligula drove round and round the ring shaking his paw at the burning statue. His shouts were drowned by the wails of the crowd and the crackle of the flames. He made three more laps before the statue of Tiberius fell. Its mighty paw crashed to the sand near the chariot and spooked the lead dogs. The chariot was flipped over like a captured mouse and Catligula was trapped underneath.

The crowd would have cheered this if they'd been watching but escape was now the only thing on their minds. Some of them managed to climb over the Arena walls but there were many who could not scale a fence, let alone balance seventy tails up in the air. Some prayed to the gods and to their ancestors that they might be delivered from the terrible judgement of the Emperor Tiberius. Others offered the gatekeepers money, as if anyone could buy their way to the front of the queue in the middle of a disaster. Where were the Spraetorian guards when they were needed? Off mousing in the woods most likely!

But Fortune still had a couple of spins left. A dry summer wind was blowing, as we often have around the Ides of Purrcury. Sparks from the headless stump of Tibbles' statue blew towards the Arena's canvas roof. Seeing what was likely to happen, a Spraetorian gave the order to haul in the shade. This is a retractable invention made of cloth that sheltered the crowds from the heat of the afternoon sun. In vain, guards and spectators tried to pull in the canvas roof, but even as they took hold of the ropes, the fire was spreading out of control. There was little anyone could do now but run from the stands into the ring itself, and take cover from the blaze.

I now made my first decision since being given my freedom. I decided that in times of such public crisis, it was every freedcat for himself! I took leave of the Imperials on the platform and searched for my friends in the crowd. When I glanced back, I saw that soon the platform itself would be lost in flames. Only Mewlia remained, flanked by a couple of bodyguards, refusing to move. She sat staring at the smashed chariot and the fallen statue. She commanded the guards to look for Catligula in the wreckage but they pretended not to hear her. Later the Purrmanians would claim that they had been ordered not to leave her side whatever happened.

Mewlia pleaded for someone to search for her dear grandson. No one wanted to approach the wreckage of the smashed chariot. Perhaps this was for fear of the dead, perhaps for fear of the living.

For reasons I cannot explain, I found myself running across the sand towards the wreckage. Perhaps I wanted to see if there was any hope for the ill-fated driver. In the press of the crowd a familiar voice called my name. It was Fleetus, my driving instructor. Together we made our way to the wreckage. It wasn't difficult to get through the crowds, everyone stood back from that doomed chariot, as if there was a curse upon it. Fleetus later told me that his only thoughts were for his dogs, for he loved them as if they were his own family. There was no saving the lead dogs. They had been crushed by the flaming wreckage and now ran wherever dead dogs run. The other four were cowering and straining at their leashes, still held fast to the burning wreckage of the overturned rig. When they saw Fleetus they recognised him immediately and became calmer. In a short time he had them free.

Without a second glance, Fleetus began to lead them away from the wreckage. I called for him to wait. He was surprised at my plan and not sure it was a good one.

'We could do as you say, but what if this was pawtent?'

I said that if it were a pawtent then nothing we could do would change Catligula's fate. Perhaps we were meant to help?

I remember his exact words: 'No good will come of this Spartapuss.'

164

Yet Fleetus could not bear to see any living thing suffer, and perhaps that is why he changed his mind. Soon the team was lashed to the wreckage and under Fleetus' command they pulled hard to try to right the overturned chariot. Seeing this, some of the crowd began to hiss and spit at us. Why were we freeing the one who had brought this destruction down upon them? I feared that Fleetus' prediction might have come true immediately but, thank Mewpiter, they were too frightened of the dogs to approach us. The team strained and slowly, the overturned rig was rolled upright. Curled up underneath the axle, and still wearing his palm crown, was the driver.

When the crowd caught sight of Catligula, they flew into a wild rage. I thought that dogs or no dogs, we would soon be torn to pieces when an almighty wail went up from our attackers. A shadow had fallen across the sun. The midday sky had turned black. But the shadow was moving, with the beat of a thousand wings.

Some in the crowd began to point to the heavens in wonder. Others threw themselves to the ground and tried to bury their faces in the sand. They were caught between the flames and whatever this terrible judgement might be.

Through this chaos, I heard a voice calling for me: 'Spartapuss! Spartapuss!'

It had the authority of Mewpiter himself. Then I was knocked over, as if by a thunderbolt. When I came to my senses, Russell apologised for making a mess of his landing. He had come as fast as he could, and I saw that he was at the head of an enormous flock of crows, their wings blocking out the sun.

Working in teams, our rescuers picked us up by the scruffs of our necks and flew us out of reach of the flames.

Fleetus and myself were amongst the first to be rescued and afterwards Katrin and Cleocatra. Russell and his fellows did not rest until every living cat was safely out of the Arena, saving hundreds of lives.

And so the tale of the Games of Purrcury is told, or at least the tale of my part in the day's events. Many worked through day and night to ensure that the fire did not spread out of the Arena and through the city. Rome owes our own dear Katrin a great debt, for it was her idea that we could stop the blaze spreading by diverting the stream from the spa.

CATILIS XVIII

July 18th

Free, but not Free Born

NOW I MUST take up my pen again, or I may forget the habit of writing. There is much to record, especially about politics and gossip. As a freedcat, I fear that I shall have little more interest in politics than when I was a slave. Unlike the free born, we freedcats cannot vote in the elections. However, I can attend the Forum, and my ears are as sharp as any free-born cat's.

Today I heard that the Emperor Tiberius has sent word from Capri and has abolished the No-Ped laws. There wasn't a great celebration when we heard this news. Many thought that it was a trick to see if any more No-Peds would reveal themselves by celebrating. But it wasn't a trick: the No-Ped laws are gone. And the Emperor Tibbles has banned all games, circus shows and wild beast hunts, until the repair of his statue and the rebuilding of the Arena have been paid for in full. Senator Pusspero shall lead an enquiry into the causes of the fire.

The Senate can beg as much as they like, but Tibbles will not return from Capri. He says he is busy redecorating his holiday villa. He has promised to appoint a new governor to rule Rome in his place. But it is said that he has fallen out with Mewlia.

As for Catligula, little has been heard of him. It is said that Mewlia has him locked up in a basket in the palace, attended by the finest doctors from all corners of the Empire.

I have much to thank the Emperor for, he has ordered that all debts must be paid. I have not yet received from Clawdius the sum of five hundred gold coins that was granted to me but, with the help of my friends, we have collected enough to buy Kitus his freedom and get him released from gladiator school. Nothing has been heard of his brother Katus since his disappearance from the Arena.

Otherwise, I do not have much news to report for I am not at Spatopia as much as I was before my arrest. Here at Bathhausia, they are very polite and well organised. They have a Welcome Pack of instructions for new members. I got about halfway through their Forbidden Behaviours list last night before nodding off on the kitchen steps. As it happens this was an illegal place to sleep, covered in section VII. I have received an official warning.

CATILIS XIX

July 19th

A Feast at Bathhausia

RUSSELL AND I have just returned from a joint celebration that was given in our honour at the public's expense. They were going to hold it in

Spatopia but Mogullania offered Clawdius' apologies saying that the complex is now closed whilst undergoing complete refurbishment. After some consideration, Katrin decided to have the party here in the feasting hall of Bathhausia. They have gone out of their way to make a fine feast for all of us and even allowed Katrin full use of the kitchens. After she had completed all the necessary paperwork, she cooked me my favourite dish of spiced chicken.

Everyone was beautifully groomed for the occasion. Cleocatra the cleaner was a particular surprise. She wore a splendid blue patterned collar with a golden coin set at the front. As it glittered in the torchlight, I recognised the strange characters on the reverse of the coin. I have seen that writing before, on the coin that Tefnut gave me on my final day of training. Cleocatra approached me and whispered in my ear:

'Tefnut sends her congratulations. She is sorry she cannot be here, she must attend to other matters. Your friend Katus is safe.'

Before I could make any reply, Katrin called for silence. I was presented with a silver bowl on which Cursus had engraved:

SPAR TA PUSS DRINK HERE FREE

Or at least, I trust it was Cursus that engraved it, judging by the misspelling of my name.

After the meal, I made a short speech. Having thanked each of my friends in turn, my thoughts turned to my old master, Clawdius. I said that it was a shame that my noble 'friend in high places' could not be here tonight. Katrin looked surprised at this and replied that he was here, standing right next to me. It seems that I had got it wrong. The friend had been Russell, not Clawdius, and 'high places' was a hint about their plan to fly me out of the Arena (in case the pardon did not arrive in time).

As it turned out, Fortune spun things so that Russell and his flock arrived late, only to find the Arena in flames.

I smiled at this and thanked my friend again for everything he'd done.

I cannot help wondering about Clawdius. I had been his loyal servant for many years but he had done nothing to help me when I was arrested. Now he owed me a large sum of money, which he showed no sign of paying. He had refused us the use of Spatopia for my celebration and he'd not said a word to me since my imprisonment. He had proved himself to be no friend of mine in any of his actions. Yet with all my heart, I would have had him with me here tonight. Perhaps all of this is pawtent. We cannot see the whole cloth that Fortune weaves, we can only follow our own thread.

It was thoroughly dark when Russell, Katrin and I returned to Spatopia. We three sat late into the night on Katrin's steps and gazed at the stars, wondering about the bowl of the world, what lies beyond the ocean, how to find the Land of the Dead and other such matters. Then we were startled by a frightening howl. It was so loud that I nearly scaled the wall before I knew what had happened.

'Perhaps they've let Catligula out of his basket,' said Russell.

Then we caught a whiff of a familiar scent drifting downwind.

'The wild beasts are back,' said Katrin.

The Spartapuss series is set in ancient Rome, in a world ruled by cats.

I Am Spartapuss
BOOK I

Spartapuss, a ginger cat, is happy managing Rome's most famous Bath & Spa. But Fortune has other plans for him.
ISBN: 9781906132422

Catligula
BOOK II

When Catligula becomes Emperor, his madness brings Rome to within a whisker of disaster.
ISBN: 9781906132484

Die Clawdius
BOOK III

The Emperor Clawdius decides to invade Spartapuss' home – The Land of the Kitons.
ISBN: 9780954657680

Boudicat
BOOK IV

Queen Boudicat has declared war on Rome and she wants Spartapuss to join her rebel army.
ISBN: 9781906132019

Cleocatra's Kushion
BOOK V

Spartapuss must travel through Fleagypt to the land of the Kushites and find his missing son.
ISBN: 9781906132064

www.mogzilla.co.uk/shop
www.spartapuss.co.uk

CATLIGULA

By Robin Price

'*Was this the most unkindest cat of all?*'

In the second adventure in the Spartapuss series...

Catligula becomes Emperor and his madness brings Rome
to within a whisker of disaster. When Spartapuss gets a job
at the Imperial Palace, Catligula wants him as his new best
friend. The Spraetorian Guard hatch a plot to destroy this
power-crazed puss in an Arena ambush. Will Spartapuss go
through with it, or will our six-clawed hero become history?

"...the descriptions of life in classical Rome are good,
particularly the set piece in the Arena...Readers who know
the original stories will enjoy the fun, and those who don't
know the history may be enticed to look more closely at the
Roman stories."– THE SCHOOL LIBRARIAN

ISBN 9781906132484

THE OLYMPUSS GAMES

Follow the adventures of the Son of Spartapuss and his fiery companion Furia from gladiator school to Mount Olympuss.

Book I: Son of Spartapuss
ISBN: 9781906132811 £6.99

Artwork by Chris Watson

THE OLYMPUSS GAMES

Follow the adventures of Son of Spartapuss and his fiery companion Furia from gladiator school to the foot of Mount Olympuss.

SON OF SPARTAPUSS
BOOK I
New to Rome, the son of Spartapuss has a lot to learn. When a mysterious stranger pays his debts he finds himself in a school for gladiators.
ISBN: 9781906132811

EYE OF THE CYCLAW
BOOK II
The Son of Spartapuss learns Furia is on a secret quest to Mount Olympuss. But to qualify for the games they must defeat the awesome Cyclaw.
ISBN: 9781906132835

MAZE OF THE MINOPAW
BOOK III
On route to the Olympuss Games, the Son of Spartapuss and Furia get mixed up in an ancient mystery. Can they escape from the maze of the Minopaw?
ISBN: 9781906132842

STARS OF OLYMPUSS
BOOK IV
To complete the quest our heroes must defeat two deadly enemies: the fearsome Furburrus and the monstrous Mewdussa!
ISBN: 9781906132828

BUY BOOKS AT WWW.MOGZILLA.CO.UK/SHOP

JOIN THE FELINE EMPIRE AT
WWW.SPARTAPUSS.CO.UK

Attention!

Write your own epic stories
at

www.creativewritingclub.co.uk

Message ends.